Y

THAT

TO

MY

FACE

CANCELLED

D0794861

Say That To My Face

DAVID PRETE

FOURTH ESTATE • *London* and *New York*

CITY OF LIMERICK
98436
PUBLIC LIBRARY

First published in Great Britain in 2004
by Fourth Estate
A division of HarperCollins*Publishers*
77–85 Fulham Palace Road,
Hammersmith, London W6 8JB

9 8 7 6 5 4 3 2 1

First published in the US by W.W. Norton 2003

Copyright © David Prete 2003

The right of David Prete to be identified as the author
of this work has been asserted by him in accordance with
the Copyright, Designs and Patents Act 1988

ISBN 0 00 7179324

Typeset in Aldine 401

Printed and bound in Great Britain by
Clays Ltd, St Ives plc

All rights reserved. No part of this publication may be
reproduced, stored in a retrieval system, or transmitted,
in any form or by any means, electronic, mechanical,
photocopying, recording or otherwise, without the prior
permission of the publishers.

This book is sold subject to the condition that it shall not,
by way of trade or otherwise, be lent, re-sold, hired out or
otherwise circulated without the publisher's prior consent
in any form of binding or cover other than that in which it
is published and without a similar condition including this
condition being imposed on the subsequent purchaser.

FOR MY SISTER

Were it possible for us to see further than our knowledge reaches, and yet a little way beyond the outworks of our divining, perhaps we would endure our sadnesses with greater confidence than our joys. For they are the moments when something new has entered into us, something unknown; our feelings grow mute in shy perplexity, everything in us withdraws, a stillness comes, and the new, which no one knows, stands in the midst of it and is silent.

—*Rainer Maria Rilke*

CONTENTS

ACKNOWLEDGMENTS

My deepest gratitude goes to:

Alane Mason for believing this book could fly and giving it the tailwind it needed.

Sarah Chalfant for the simplicity and grace with which your help comes.

Gary and Bruno, have cash, will travel. Liz DeGiglio, your ice skate left the most treasured mark. Brian Prager, you'll never be old to me. Z for offering your gut. Alex Lyras for your invaluable input on the early drafts and all-around inspiration. Bobby B. Sarahji. Sabrina and Tracy. Shannon K. Aunt Mary, Uncle Ronnie and all of the extended family. George and Mike for teaching me, among other things, how to tell a story.

Angie, Jerry and Pat Castaldo for helping to create a beautiful first home. My parents and their two perfect hearts. Also, Donna and Lee. My greatest confidant, my sister.

To the Hands that were on mine while this was written. And to all who entered with a punch or a kiss and exited with a scream or a whisper, I still hear you and feel you.

Finally, the courage and love brought to my life, that is so Big, just floors me.

SAY
THAT
TO
MY
FACE

This was the part of the ride I loved the best. It was my part. When I got up to a good speed and pulled the skid brake, it made the back wheels of my Big Wheel lock and kick out to one side, which sent me into a spin and then a stop. If I got scared and tried to stop the spin with my limbs, chances were I'd get hurt: I could scrape up my feet or tip myself and go shitcan-over-teakettle onto the pavement. Either way, if I tried to stop what it was I had gotten myself into, I'd end up face-ass down on the street.

At four and a half, as I would fall asleep, I'd remember the rides I took that day. I could feel the motion of the skids playing themselves over in me as I lay in bed. Like spending the whole day in the ocean and that same night still feeling the waves going back and forth in my body as if the tide got stuck there. I'd hear the sound of the plastic tire grinding against the asphalt and feel my eyes watering from the wind. It was simply the best thing that ever happened to a kid since the beginning of kids. That's what I thought about in my fifth year when I would fall asleep.

The other thing I would think about was why there were four different homes in which I was falling asleep.

———

WHEN MY PARENTS were married they lived in the Bronx. When they got divorced it was decided that my mother, my sister and I would move a few miles north, into my grandparents' house in Yonkers. My mom was twenty-one years old and broke. Her parents' house was small, so my sister, my mother and I shared a bedroom. It was a converted attic with a pitched roof and a crawlspace behind one of the walls. Just big enough for three beds and three dressers. The one decorative touch was an almost-life-size poster of Robert Redford playing the Sundance Kid. Our mother hung the poster directly over the headboard of her bed. We lived in that house with our grandparents from when I was one year old until I was six.

The address was 15 Verona Avenue. Verona Avenue was a long and steep hill. The bottom of the hill intersected Central Park Avenue, which was a major six-lane roadway that ran through all of Yonkers. During a hard rainstorm the water would come down that hill and overflow the gutters. That's when my sister and I put plastic bags over our sneakers and splashed around in what all the adults were cursing the city about.

After dinner, before we would go to bed, I'd get up on my grandfather's lap. Everyone knew what that meant. My grandfather would yell playfully but really loud, "*Get the hell outta here! Now I gotta scratch his back?*"

I'd play like he really wasn't going to. "Ah, Gramps, come oooooooon."

Then he'd slap me on the back and shake his head at me as if to say, *Look at the prince here,* sit me on his lap and scratch. We had a pretty smooth routine.

My grandfather was the best back-scratcher I ever knew. The guy was a butcher. He worked with his hands. He understood the force of cleaving and the subtlety of carving. He had thick heavy fingernails, which he kept very well. They were perfect for our routine. He had his clipper and nail buffer (not a file, a two-sided nail buffer), which he kept on his nightstand right next to the whetstone he used to sharpen his butcher's knives. He took as good care of his nails as he did all of his tools.

There was also a paved walkway that ran from the front of the house all the way to the back, eventually connecting to the back patio. Hugging this walkway was a fence that separated my grandparents' house from their neighbors'. This walkway was a long enough strip for me to get some pretty good speed on my Big Wheel and hit some nice spins. If ever I rode to the front of the house my mother would yell, "Stay away from the street!" then mumble to herself, "That Big Wheel scares the shit out of me."

The house at 15 Verona Avenue was where I would fall asleep during most weekdays. House Number One.

If I wasn't there on a weeknight, it was because I went with my sister to sleep at House Number Two—Aunt Marie and Uncle Ernie's place. They had two daughters, our cousins, Dina and Vicky. They were not our blood relations. They were self-declared family, friends from the Bronx who were so close they needed to be deemed Aunt, Uncle and Cousin. My mother and my Aunt Marie had known each other since grade school. They got married about the same time, had kids about the same time and moved not only to the same neighborhood in the Bronx, but to the same block. We lived at 2224 Grace Avenue; they lived at 2216 Grace Avenue. Some nights, if we were playing at the other family's house and we happened to fall asleep on their couch, our parents would just leave us there until morning. We got breakfast no matter where we woke up. I guess they were better than family. When we moved to Yonkers, my mother would drive us down to the Bronx and Aunt Marie and Uncle Ernie would take us in for the night. This happened about once a week. Our grandparents' house didn't lack love, but nonetheless my sister and I often gravitated back to Grace Avenue. Maybe we were leaning toward a type of normalcy or honoring a need we felt for some kind of completion. They had a house with a mother, a father and two kids. We couldn't get enough of it.

House Number Three was actually an apartment. It belonged to my father. And then there was his girlfriend's apartment. My father saw my sister and me on weekends. That was the custody agreement. Saturday nights we either slept at his apartment in Port Chester (another suburb about twenty minutes from Yonkers) or we would go to his girlfriend's place, where my sister and I would crash on a pull-out couch. House Number Four.

I HAD TROUBLE sleeping at that age regardless of where I slept. I never wanted to go to bed for fear that I would miss something. I remember lying in bed hearing adults talking or a newspaper turning or the television and I thought, *I gotta get out there. What could they possibly be doing? There is definitely something goin' on.*

The other thing that would keep me awake was the sound of my parents' voices. The ones that my mind recorded from when they were still married. Not conversations. Fights. And not the words they used to fight with but the sounds they produced while they were fighting. Theirs was not an amicable breakup. There's a thing that happens to a person's voice at the peak of rage. Vocal cords no longer become a free channel to express emotion. Vibrations become impeded and grate against the inside of one's throat. This is what I knew to be the sound of my parents' relationship ending. When that recorded noise would keep me awake, I would try to replace it with the sound of my Big Wheel. A plastic tire rolling over cement. This worked for me sometimes.

Even after I fell asleep, I didn't easily stay asleep. I would often wake up in the night, usually from nightmares. And sometimes figments of my dreams would float around the room. This was terrifying, and the only way I knew how to snap myself completely out of the dream state was to run. I would run into the bathroom, down the stairs or out into the hall. Once I woke up and started running from something and crashed right into my mother's bedpost. Nose first. My mother sat me up on the bathroom sink with a wad of toilet paper on my nose to stop the bleeding. "What the hell were you doin'?"

"Umm . . . I couldn't sleep."

"So you figured you'd run into a couple of walls? Knock yourself out?"

She made me laugh. This, she was good at.

Of the four different places I slept, there was only one constant: my sister Catherine always slept right beside me. She was either in the same bed as me or in the bed right next to mine for the first six years of my life.

There was a moment in the mornings, after my sister and I woke up and before we opened our eyes, when we weren't sure which one of the four houses we'd woken up in. (If you've ever fallen asleep in your own bed with your head where your feet usually are, woken up and were so confused as to why your window was now behind you, then you get the picture.) So what my sister and I would do was keep our eyes closed and try to guess. We would try to listen for someone's voice or try to smell where we were. There was always one place out of the four where we secretly wished to be, but it was never the same place every time. It depended on our mood. And sometimes, when we really, really wanted to be in one place and woke up someplace else, it was a drag. *Oh, damn, I'm here? I wanted to be there.*

IN 1975, WHEN I was four and Catherine was six, our mother, at age twenty-five, had a job at a department store. She worked weekends and some weeknights. That way her days could be spent with her children. The couple of weeknights she had to work were tough for us. I remember us crying a lot because we didn't want our mom to leave. Our grandparents were great people, but we were already one parent short.

Not only was our mother young, she was also pretty. On weekends she would go to the beauty parlor with her friends. She always wanted to be attractive for herself, but since the divorce, and for the first time in her adult life, she also had the intention of being attractive for other guys. She started dating a few years after she and my dad split.

She brought a man to 15 Verona Avenue whose name was Raymond Canalli. He was a well-dressed guy who drove a new Cadillac Coupe de Ville and apparently was in the contracting business. Ray had pudgy fingers with three big rings. Which gave his hands a look of wealth and therefore security. I liked them. I liked them when they were holding my grandmother's silverware at the dinner table and I liked them when he patted me on the head. One night, from our bedroom window, my sister and I watched my mother walk Ray to his car. Ray had one hand on our mother's back. I liked that, too.

Our mother never stayed over at Ray's place, nor did he ever stay at our grandparents' house. Even dating was a bit tricky.

Catherine and I used to tie one end of a jump rope to the partition fence. While one of us turned the free end, the other one would jump through. One night, while my mother was out with Ray, Catherine was at the fence turning the jump rope and I was sitting at the iron table on the back patio with my grandfather. He was drinking a beer and I asked him if I could have some. He had a little more than half a beer left and gave it to me. Catherine said, "Joey, come jump with me." It was a beautiful summer night; I was drinking beer with my grandfather and had my elbows on the table; I was feeling very grown up. Playing jump rope with my sister would've interfered with how cool I was. So I just sort of shrugged one shoulder at her, said, "Maybe later," and finished the warm can of Miller High Life. It didn't agree with me. Later on that night, I wound up in the bathroom throwing up, with my grandfather sitting on the edge of the bathtub watching me. With my head in the bowl, I heard my mother come home from her date and my grandmother yelling from the kitchen, "Your father gave him a beer, now he's throwing up in there!"

My mother came into the bathroom and, having assessed the situation before she even put a foot in the door, slapped my grandfather on the back of his head, slapped me on the back of my head, and walked out shouting, "I'm gone for four hours and my son winds up knee-deep in bile?"

My grandfather laughed at that. My mother screamed some more from the kitchen. "It's funny? It's so goddamn funny that I'm twenty-five and I can't go out for one night without coming back to this? It's funny, right?"

My grandfather stopped laughing. I was wishing that I had jumped rope that night and my mother was probably thinking she shouldn't go out to dinner for a while.

AFTER ABOUT SIX months into the relationship with our mom, Ray started showing up with presents for everyone. A couple toys for us kids, an expensive piece of jewelry for our mother. Then, one Wednesday night, in the middle of August 1975, Ray Canalli brought over a little something for the house. Like two television sets. One was a twenty-one-inch color TV for the living room and the other was a portable black and white number that we could watch outside on the back patio. A big color TV? For my sister and me? It sent our heads spinning. But the portable one? Now, that was something special. Plenty of people had regular TVs, but having one you could watch from your back patio? That was something to be contested. And that was exactly what Catherine and I felt on our grandparents' patio, with our bowl of popcorn, watching our New York Yankees play on our brand-new portable television set—we were something to be contested.

That night, I woke up and, standing before me in our room, a witch was sharpening her cats' claws on a whetstone. It made sounds that should've come off a chalkboard or out of a blacksmith shop. Two hateful and unyielding forces grinding against each other that sent my four-year-old ass running. When I got halfway down the stairs, I heard some kind of clanging noises and voices ahead of me. I stopped, trapped between two scary places. I looked back up the stairs. The entrance to our room was foggy and dark. The witch wasn't following me, but I still didn't know what those noises from downstairs were, so I wasn't going anywhere. I dropped to a stair and held my blanket up to my mouth. I froze. Then the clanging in the distance began to sound familiar—ceramic cups hitting against saucers, maybe. I recognized the voices as my mother's and Ray's, coming from the kitchen. As my mind cleared, I realized they were just talking and sipping coffee. It was nothing.

"Ray, what are you doing?"

"Drinking coffee with you. What are you doing?"

"Trying to raise my kids right."

"And you are. Look how happy they were tonight."

"They were happy because of the TVs, Ray."

"Yeah, and if a little TV can make them that happy, do you have any idea what a house of their own and swimming pool could do for them?"

Did he just say . . . *swimming pool*? Now I was awake. I poked my head around the corner.

"I'm not worried about what *those things* could do to them."

"Are we gonna start with that now?"

"Yeah, we're gonna start with that now. I don't see you for ten days. I don't get to ask where you were or what you were doing. Then you show up at my parents' house on a Wednesday night with a dozen roses, a black eye and two TVs that don't have a box or a price tag between them."

"Why you wanna price tag? You wanna take 'em back to the store?"

"What store would that be, Ray?"

He laughed.

"You're a shady guy, Ray."

"That's why you like me. Admit it."

"I'm not gonna like you so hard the day they start shoving your meals through a slot."

"Tough girl here."

"That's right."

"No one is gonna be shovin' my meals through a slot."

"You don't know that."

"I know that." He punctuated that by knocking his rings on the table.

"Then I don't know that."

"I'm tellin' you."

"But Ray, you don't know. You don't, you don't and you don't."

"I know how I feel about you. That's what I know. Do *you* know how I feel about you?"

"Yes."

"Do you know how you feel about *me*?"

"Yeah." She was looking down at the table.

"Do you?"

By her chin, he brought her face up to meet his. Looking right in his eyes, she said, "Yes."

"So, then?"

My mother stared at her boyfriend longingly, then a smile broke out on her lips. Ray smiled with her. She started shaking her head.

Ray said, "So whaddaya wanna do?"

"What, are you gonna walk me down the aisle wearing concrete boots?"

There was a pause. Ray grabbed her hand and leaned in closer. "Whaddaya wanna do?"

"I wanna drink my coffee."

Carefully, I walked back up to our bedroom and stood at the side of Catherine's bed.

"Rin, wake up."

She was used to this. "What?"

"Ray wants to buy us a swimming pool."

"Who said?"

"He did. I just heard him say it to Mommy."

"Where would we put a pool?"

"In the backyard?"

"Is it small?"

"I don't know. But you know what? You know what I think? I

think it's gonna be one like they have at Sprain Brook Park, only smaller."

Up until then Catherine could've had this conversation in her sleep. But now she cleared the covers off her head and propped herself up on her elbows.

"A concrete pool?"

"Yeah, a concrete pool."

"He said that?"

"Yes. He said a concrete pool."

"No way."

"Yes way! A CONCRETE POOL!" I started punching her mattress. "A BUILT-IN, CONCRETE POOL!"

"Shhh! Stop that. What else did they say?"

"I don't know, but that would be the best thing ever." The excitement was too much for me. I jumped on my bed and started beating my face into the pillow. "That would be the best."

I pulled the covers up to my chin and held them tight. My eyes were darting all over the room and my heart was all over my chest. I looked over my mother's bed and I struggled in the dark to make out Robert Redford's face and hat.

THE NEXT DAY, my mother and Catherine were in front of the bathroom mirror. My mother had just washed Catherine's hair and was now combing it out. I was pushing a Matchbox car along the rim of the bathtub watching them. Catherine said, "Mom, are you going to marry Ray?"

My mother said, "I don't know, sweetie." She was being very careful about how to answer questions on this subject and continued, "He's a really nice man, don't you think?"

"Yeah, he is."

"What makes you ask?"

"Well, if you did marry him, would we get another house?"

"We probably would. But like I said, I don't know if Mommy will marry Ray."

"If we got another house, would I have my own room?"

"I wish you could." Her carefulness slipped away for a moment.

"And would Joey have his own room?"

Whoa. Hold on a second. This was the first I ever heard about having to sleep alone. A horrifying idea that my mother seemed to like.

"Um, yeah. I guess you could both have your own room." She drifted into a fantasy about it, then caught herself. "But listen to me, Catherine, that's not what's important. What's important is that we all stay together. Me and you and Joey. Whatever happens, the three of us have to stay together."

That night, my sister and I were jumping rope by the back patio light. Inside, we could hear our mother turning the pages of a magazine. I spoke to my sister in a whisper.

"Rin?"

"What?"

"Do you think Mommy and Ray will get married?"

She kept turning the rope even though I'd stopped jumping. "I don't know. Do you want them to?"

"Umm . . ." Now that she asked, I wasn't sure. I needed her opinion. "Do you?"

"I don't know. I just don't know anymore." She was sounding very old for her age.

We heard a car pull up to the front of the house and the kitchen chair our mother was on slid on the linoleum floor as she stood up. Catherine and I went inside. My mother spoke through the screen door. "Ray, it's kinda late."

"Yeah, I'm sorry. I saw the light on."

I scrambled to my mother's legs and said hi to him. He said, "Hey, buddy Joe. Look what I got for you." He pulled out a miniature car. "Joey, this is a 1954 Porsche. James Dean used to drive a car like this. You know who James Dean was?"

"No."

"He was the coolest movie star there was."

My mother said, "Come in for a minute," and opened the door. I grabbed the car as if it were my first meal in a week.

"What do you say, Joey?"

"Thank you, Ray."

I started to drive the car all over the living room as Ray produced a can of bubbles for Catherine. Mom said, "Joey, don't wake up your grandparents."

"How'd you like that movie the other night?"

"You drove over here just to ask me how I liked the movie we saw last week?"

"Yeah. That, and I thought maybe you could do me a favor."

"What?"

"What night did we see that movie?"

Our mother was getting a little annoyed. "Um, Wednesday. What's the—"

"Are you sure it wasn't Tuesday?"

"What are you talking about?"

"I'm talkin' about the movie we saw last Tuesday."

"You're not being cute, Ray. What's the favor?"

"I was thinking—here's the favor part—if someone was to ask you what night we saw the movie, do you think you could tell them—"

"Someone? Who is someone?"

"Joey, didn't me and your mother go see the movies last Tuesday night?"

"I don't know."

"That's a good answer, Joe. If you tell 'em nothin', they ain't got nothin' on you."

My mother cut him right off. "Joey, take your car and go upstairs. I'll be right there to put you to bed. Catherine, go with him."

I said, "Why?"

"Upstairs." There was the tone we didn't argue with. Catherine and I got halfway up the stairs when we heard our mom hiss at Ray. "Outside."

The screen door shut. Catherine and I could still hear them.

"This is not fuckin' funny, Ray. Who the hell is gonna ask me what? And why?"

"Look, look. Sorry I ever said anything about it. I didn't think it would be such a big deal."

"A big deal? You come in here, try to turn my four-year-old son into an accessory, and now—"

"I did not."

"You asked my son to lie for you, and now all of a sudden I've got 'someone' who might ask me 'something' about where you were last week. *Where* are they gonna ask me this? Are they gonna show up at my job? Are they gonna come here? To my parents' house? Where my children live, to ask me?"

"It's probably nothin'."

"It's already somethin' and I don't want it. And another thing, these kids don't need another guy to come and go."

"That's not me!"

"Oh, no?"

"No."

"Then tell me the truth, Ray. Tell me the God's honest truth, even if this thing is nothin', and it's probably not—"

"It is nothing."

"Even so, even if that's so, there'll still be somethin' else, won't there? Won't there, Ray? You'll have to leave the country or go to jail—"

"I won't."

"You don't know that. And what will happen to us? Tell me the truth right now. What will happen to us? Will anyone be able to protect us?"

"Whaddaya want me to say? That I'm sure about how the rest of my life is gonna work out? Nobody can say that. Nobody really knows what'll happen to them. And forgive me for makin' this example, but didn't you think you were gonna be married to that guy forever?"

"Go on."

"Maybe we don't know nothin' for sure about what's gonna happen to us. All I can tell you is that I know how I feel and I know what I wanna do. Don't you see what I can give you?"

"Raymond, look at me and tell me that if you made a mistake it wouldn't come down on all of us. Tell me that right now."

He took a long time to answer. "I can't."

"Then neither can I. I can't do it."

There was silence. Then the soles of Ray's shoes moved against the slate stairs and my mother said, "Raymond, don't."

A little more silence.

"I love them so much, Ray. I love them so fucking much I can't stand it sometimes."

"I know the feeling."

Last thing Catherine and I heard before we ran up the stairs was Ray's car door slam.

THE NEXT DAY, Catherine and I were in our room with our mom, packing up clothes to bring to our father's for the weekend. I just blurted it out: "Mom, are you and Ray gonna get married?"

Catherine looked at me as if I were going to get in trouble for asking that. Our mother sat on my bed and said, "Me and Ray are not getting married." We were silent. We knew there was more. "Also, I don't think Ray is gonna be comin' over to the house anymore."

Catherine said, "He's not?"

"No, he's not, Catherine."

Then I asked the question that our mother was dreading. "Why?"

She couldn't explain it to us. She couldn't explain to us why Ray wasn't coming back. She couldn't explain to us why there had been a divorce. She couldn't explain what brought people together, then led them apart. In that moment—sitting on a bed in her parents' converted attic, at twenty-five years old, with her two children—she had no idea why. She grabbed my arm. "Oh, sweetie"—her eyes got still, she seemed to be looking inside herself for more words—"I didn't want him to." Then her head dropped and her face distorted into extreme sadness. It happened as fast as you could tilt a hologram and see a different picture. Her head landed in her hands. My sister and I had that stunned silence that kids get when they see their parents fall apart. We might as well have just watched a car crash. We stood there not even blinking, in awe of a crying mother. Then we heard the beep of a horn. She took a deep breath, wiped her nose on her forearm and said, "There's your father. Don't keep him waiting." I climbed up on the bed and gave her a kiss goodbye, then Catherine did the same. Our mother picked up our bag and followed Catherine and me down the stairs. From behind the screen door she watched her children get into her ex-husband's car and drive away.

THAT NIGHT WE slept at our father's girlfriend's house. I asked Catherine where she thought Ray was. She didn't know. We were trying to figure out a few things: why we had come so close and now had nothing to show for it but two television sets, and what was going to happen now. Sometime during the conversation I started to cry. Catherine tried to get me to think of my Big Wheel, but I just cried harder. Our father heard me and came into the room. He was puzzled and looked at my sister.

"What's the matter with your brother?"

"He can't sleep."

"Why not?"

"I don't know."

Then he asked me, "Joey, what's the matter?"

"I can't sleep."

"Why not?"

"I don't know."

My sister chimed in, "Tell him to think of his Big Wheel." She was trying to help him help me. She was smart.

"Your Big Wheel? What about your Big Wheel?"

I didn't answer.

My sister said, "He likes to think about his Big Wheel. It helps him sleep."

Realizing Catherine knew more about this than he did, our father said, "You wanna think of your Big Wheel?"

"Yeah."

"Well, how does your Big Wheel go? What does it sound like?"

I said, "It sounds like . . . I don't know."

My father started to make car sounds. Honking horns and everything. My sister rolled her eyes. She knew this wasn't going very well.

"Come on, Joey, how does a Big Wheel go? Does it go like this: *brrruuummm*. Or, *vruuummm*. Or like, *beep-beep*."

I just stared at him. How, as a four-year-old, could I say, *It sounds like the merciful palm of the Lord, soothing all my unspeakable childhood angst and misery. Can you make* that *sound, Dad?*

"How does it go, Joey?"

"It just goes."

I was dismissive enough about it that my father knew he had to change gears.

"Hey," he said. The timbre in his voice changed. He pushed my sister and me closer together. "You guys know Credence Clearwater Revival?"

"No. What's that?"

"It's a rock and roll band and they have a song about Big Wheels."

He had my interest. I said, "They do?"

"Yeah, they do. I'm not kiddin' you."

"How does it go?" I asked.

"Here. It goes like this."

With his head hovering over mine, he started to sing, a soft ballad rendition of "Proud Mary." He didn't quite hit all the notes, but he knew every word. He sang about how I shouldn't lose sleep worrying about how things might turn out. And about how there was a river somewhere with people who knew how to live. They all rode big wheels. If you went there, it didn't matter if you were poor or sad or alone because these river people were happy to give. And there was a fiery woman there named Proud Mary. The chorus of the song played like a mantra in my head and faded me out to sleep. Big wheels keep on turnin' . . . big wheels keep on turnin' . . . big wheels keep on turnin'.

THAT SUNDAY AFTERNOON, Catherine and I came back to Verona Avenue with a firm agenda. "Mom," Catherine said. "We want to sleep at Aunt Marie and Uncle Ernie's tonight."

"Listen, I wanted to talk to you kids about that."

That sentence was death. There was a certain tone our mother used when she was about to spring bad news on us. As soon as we heard it, we tried to cover our ears with our shoulders.

"Catherine is going to be starting kindergarten in a few weeks . . ."

And there was the other tone. The everything-is-going-to-be-all-right tone that not even our mother believed. This was bad. ". . . and that means that she has to be in school in the morning. And Uncle Ernie has to go to work and Aunt Marie can't drive all the way up from the Bronx and take you to school, sweetie. So you kids can't sleep over there anymore."

I said, "Can't they sleep over here?"

"No, they can't, Joey."

This was really friggin' bad. In three days, we lost a potential stepfather, a swimming pool and four immediate family members. Not to mention two houses—the dream home Raymond was going to give us, and the one Aunt Marie and Uncle Ernie already had given us.

That night, before dinner, I took my Big Wheel out for a ride. I spun out a few times along the side of the house, but that wasn't helping me out of the state I was in. I rode to the front of the house and sat there on my low-rider plastic tricycle. I stared at the street. My eyes defocused on the asphalt. For a moment, my mind became empty, until a green car came down the hill of Verona Avenue and broke my stillness. I watched it the whole time it idled at the intersection. When the light changed, it took a left on Central Park Avenue and I followed it with my eyes until it was out of my sight. I looked up the hill it had come from, looked back at my grandparents' house, stood up and carried my Big Wheel four house-lengths up the hill.

As soon as I got on the seat, I started to roll down the hill. I wasn't ready for that. I tried to stop the front tire from turning by jamming my feet on the pedals. And I did stop it. But the decline was so steep, I started to skid down the hill anyway. This, I couldn't stop. I looked to the bottom of the hill and saw the cars going by on the avenue. Holy shit. I started to pedal in order to stop the skid, but soon I couldn't keep up with the speed of the wheel. I took my feet off the pedals and that's when I understood the power of gravity. The wind got loud in my ears. I looked down. The pavement was a gray and black blur and the pedals were rotating as fast as pistons in a car engine. My eyes were tearing. From the wind, I think. And when I crossed the last driveway before the intersection I pulled that brake harder than I'd pulled anything in the past four years and sent myself into a spin of more than two complete revolutions before I stopped.

In my dizziness, I could see my mother running at me. The traffic light behind her turned red, and made her hair look like it was in flames. I thought the ride I just took was scary, but I didn't know the true meaning of fear until I looked into her face. The only questions she had for me pertained directly to my sanity. "Are you crazy? You almost got yourself killed!" With one hand she held the Big Wheel off the ground and with the other hand hit me on my ass. The slaps came in conjunction with the words she emphasized. "HOW could you DO such a STUPID THING?" She dragged me into the backyard. "That's it! You're not riding this friggin' thing ever again! You hear me? EVER!"

I sat on the walkway crying, as my mother went into the house

CITY OF LIMERICK
PUBLIC LIBRARY
98436

and then returned with a rope. In pure horror, I watched her tie my Big Wheel to the fence that separated the houses. "And you're never goin' in the street, either. OK? Now get off the floor, clean yourself up and get in here and eat dinner!" Then she slammed the door.

My sister, who had been watching this whole scene from the patio, decided it was better to say nothing and slowly went in the house and sat at the kitchen table. I couldn't stop crying. I looked over to my favorite toy. Not only had she tied it up, but she left it lying on its side. It looked like an injured animal about to die in captivity.

That night, we sat through the quietest dinner in our family's history. There was no yelling about how much room the neighbors' cars were taking up on the street or about how we needed to finish chewing before we spoke. Or about clogged gutters. There was no talk about how good the food was or if we wanted more. And there was no back-scratching afterward. When we finished, Catherine and I watched TV on the patio until our mother came outside and said, "It's time to go to sleep."

I lay in my bed for a long time listening to the adults coursing through the end of their night. Catherine knew I was still awake.

"I'm sorry I have to go to kindergarten," she said.

"It's OK."

"I don't wanna go."

"You'll have fun."

"I don't know."

A LITTLE WHILE later, I woke up and saw a king flipping a gold coin in the air. He caught it and slapped it on his wrist like he was calling heads or tails. He pointed to the window. I went to it and looked down. There was Ray standing on the back patio holding a puppy. I turned back and caught the last moment of the king's robe as he left the room and started down the stairs. My mother was asleep in her bed. I grabbed my blanket and went down the staircase. At the bottom, I turned left toward my grandparents' room. Through their doorframe, they looked like a Dr. Seuss illustration—stick legs and two bulging stomachs under a cover. In the hall was a pair of shoes with nothing in them. In the kitchen, dinner dishes were on a drying rack, looking like they were about to move by themselves. The only background noise was the hum of the refrigerator.

I walked out the back door, onto the patio. There was no Ray, no king, no puppy. Just my Big Wheel still on its side. I went over and stood it upright. I lay down next to it, put my head on the seat and pulled my blanket over me. I was tired. I wanted to sleep. But I wanted something more. What I really wanted was an all-inclusive sleepover party. And when I shut my eyes, I saw everyone I wanted to invite. A picture came to me of my dad singing to me. My mother was giving me a bath and my grandfather was carving a turkey. My grandmother was dumping pasta in a colander. I saw my Cousin Dina on a swing and Vicky was trying to tie her shoe. Aunt Marie and Uncle Ernie were at their dinner table and Ray was driving in his Cadillac. Catherine was sleeping right beside me. Also, there was a swimming pool.

I don't know how long I had been asleep. My body jumped when I woke up. I didn't open my eyes. I could tell it was still dark. An occasional car drove down Central Park Avenue. It was summertime and it was quiet. The patio smelled of dampness. The pictures of my family were still appearing in me. I felt the plastic seat of my Big Wheel under my head. I kept my eyes closed, but knew exactly where I was.

NOT BECAUSE I'M THIRSTY

The theory is this: The way in which we tried to get the attention of the first person we ever had a crush on is the way we continue to do it for the rest of our lives. However creative, desperate, blunt or devious our young tactics were, we don't give them up.

My tactic? Pretended I was a superhero. Pretended I had enough superpowers to rescue people from the ordinary world, that I came from a place better than earth, where superhuman things are a way of life. A faraway place, where magical powers are realized and saviors are born. Who wouldn't fall in love with someone from that world?

So, that's what I tried to convince the first girl I had a crush on—that I was different than the rest. That I had powers no one she knew would ever have.

When I was twenty-six I told my girlfriend about this theory—that as adults we still try to win lovers with our childhood tactics—and what my tactics were. "Yeah," she said, "that *is* what you do, isn't it?"

But I don't want to talk about that. I want to talk about the year I was in the second grade. The year there were regular kickball games up the block and a crazy guy going around New York killing people. I want to talk about the first girl who let me be a superhero.

EVERY NIGHT IN front of the Gallaghers' house, a kickball game would start up. A group of neighborhood kids gathered there after dinner and, in place of doing homework, played ball. The kickball season began in early spring and ended when we started having to run the bases with our hands in our pockets. My sister Catherine and I walked the five doors down to the Gallaghers' and played until dusk, when our mother would call us home.

Mr. and Mrs. Gallagher didn't run the kind of house in which the neighborhood kids were invited inside all the time. We didn't even know what the inside of their house looked like—never got closer than the curb. Mr. Gallagher would only pop his head out the front door every so often to tell us to keep it down because his wife wasn't feeling well and she was trying to sleep. I don't ever remember actually seeing Mrs. Gallagher. But the manhole cover in front of their driveway was the best natural home plate on the block.

Rory Gallagher had long brown hair. Of the five Gallagher kids, she was second youngest. She stood with hands on her waist and her bony hip kicked out to one side. She also had a habit—which she didn't pick up from her older brothers—of spitting. With a low growl she would collect the saliva in her throat, then hock it onto the street, two feet from where you were standing. It got so we didn't mind. The only time Rory ever caught grief for this was when she spit on the street during the kickball games. If someone fielded a ball that had rolled over one of Rory's saliva patches, they wouldn't try to get the runner out; they would run after her and try to wipe the ball on her.

I once got my nerve up enough to ask her why she spit all the time. She claimed she only spit after she ate chicken cutlets for dinner, because she hated the aftertaste.

It was Rory's attention I was trying to get.

BATMAN WAS A superhero who was also human. When he was a little kid, Batman's parents were murdered. To avenge their murder and fight crime of all kinds, Batman developed all the strength and skill of his mind and body beyond traditional limits. He didn't get an overdose of gamma radiation or get bit by a spider in a lab experiment, nor could he breathe underwater, turn invisible or assume different miraculous forms. Yeah, he could scale walls and kick bad-guy ass like the rest of the superheroes, but ultimately, he was just an ordinary man making the best of what he had, fighting for his cause.

Every so often during the kickball games I would have to run back home when I heard the Batphone ring. A call from the police commissioner saying there was a problem the cops couldn't handle without me. I'd run back to the game and announce that I had to get to an undisclosed location immediately to fight crime. I'd apologize to Rory for having to leave, but demonstrate a superhero's generosity by leaving my own kickball behind so the game could continue without me. In that case my sister would bring the ball home and I wouldn't catch hell from Mom for losing it. And it wasn't easy to part with my ball. I was six. It was my ball.

There were times when I was able to handle the crime situation over the phone. In which case I would walk back up the street, assure everyone that everything was going to be all right, and I'd finish out the game.

When it was time to go home, our mother belted out our names from the front stoop like an ocean liner's horn wailing during a launch. And if you missed the boat, you were in trouble. If you missed it during that particular kickball season, which started March of 1977, you were in an extraordinary amount of trouble.

YOUNG GIRLS WITH shoulder-length brown hair. That's who we were told he went after.

"Under no circumstances do you kids go out when it's dark out. Do you hear me?"

"How about if the ice cream man comes?"

"No. There's ice cream in the refrigerator."

The first murder happened in July of the previous year. Initially it was just another homicide, a story that took up a tiny space in the newspaper. But March 8, 1977, marked the fifth attack. By then he had gone after nine people. Then it drew a lot of attention. Sketches of him were on TV, in the paper, posted in Laundromats and on telephone poles everywhere. He looked as plain as anyone's father. Except he scared the shit out of us.

"Mom, does he only go after people in the city?"

"They don't know. He goes after people in the Bronx, where we used to live, and that's only ten minutes away from where we live now. I want you to listen to me. If you see a yellow or a cream-colored car with a man in it, I want you to run away from it. You run home and you tell me. Do you understand?"

They were shot in parked cars, on their front porches or walking home from school. The cops knew it was the same guy because they were able to confirm all the bullets came from the same kind of gun—a .44-caliber revolver. That's how he got his first name, which all the kids in my neighborhood called him: the .44-Caliber Killer.

"They said he hates women. And you know how the cops know he's gonna do it again?"

"How?"

"Because his gun holds five bullets and he only shoots four of them. He keeps one for the next time."

"That's not true."

"That's what my dad said."

"No, he keeps one bullet in his gun in case someone tries to run after him and catch him, then he can shoot them, too."

He started to leave notes for the cops, poems about pouring lead on girls' heads until they were dead, cats mating and birds singing. He also left drawings with circles and arrows and crosses that looked like the insignia of demonic worship. He called himself "the monster" and signed the notes with his second name: Son of Sam.

My sister once walked around the house with yellow guck in her hair and a cellophane bag over it for about an hour. Then my mother leaned her backward over the kitchen sink and washed the guck out. When my sister lifted her head up, her brown hair was now blond.

My mother was very excited. "Oh, look how pretty. Come look at yourself."

I followed them into the bathroom. Mom sat Catherine up on the sink in front of the mirror for a second opinion.

"Catherine, it's so pretty. You look like a movie star."

Catherine touched her hair the way a kid fumbles with a new toy, not sure how it works.

"Do you like it, sweetie?"

My sister smiled. "Yeah. I like it a lot."

WHEN I ASKED my mother how Mrs. Gallagher died, she told me she was sick with cancer. I was in the second grade; Rory was in the fifth. It happened in April, only a month after the fifth Son of Sam attack.

After the funeral, family, friends and people from the neighborhood went over to the Gallaghers' house. It was the only time I ever saw it from the inside. For us kids, having to sit quietly in their strange house with a group of adults, in our nice clothes, with no game going on outside was the most disorienting part of the whole day. What I really wanted to do was poke around in their kitchen and bathroom and definitely get a look at Rory's room.

I think I was the only one who noticed Rory walk up the stairs. I followed her. All the doors that lined the long hallway were closed; the daylight couldn't get in. Rory opened the last door on the right and went in. I knew I was in a place I probably shouldn't have been, but curiosity coupled with my crush kept me going. The power to turn invisible would have come in handy. I peeked in after her. The room had a huge canopy bed and two layers of curtains on the windows. Against the wall was a vanity covered with makeup cases and bottles of perfume like my mother had in her room. Also, there were bottles just like the ones my step-father kept his asthma medicine in.

Rory opened a dresser drawer and was kneeling in front of it, her hands kneading through the clothes. She looked confused. She searched through the drawer as if what she wanted was there last time she checked. She took a green sweater out and held it up by the sleeves, but still wasn't satisfied with what she found. Maybe Rory believed that she couldn't have been brought to a scary place such as this earth only to be left unattended, and was convinced that folded up in that sweater she would find a perfect explanation for all this. She examined the whole thing, then reached inside and carefully read the label.

I forgot I was trying to be unnoticed and said, "What's it say?"

My voice or my presence didn't startle her. She seemed to know I was there the whole time. She turned her head to me; the sweater was draped over her lap.

"It says you can't wash it."

BETWEEN THE FIVE children in mourning and parents who were afraid to let their children out of the house, our kickball games really slowed down. A few of us would still gather in front of the Gallaghers' house but felt we didn't have the right to the playing field unless one of the Gallagher kids joined us. When they didn't come out, we just stood around, bounced the ball around for a while, then reluctantly went back home way before the sun went down. And when one of them did come out to start the game, it was never Rory. She stopped playing altogether, and without her around there wasn't much crime for me to fight.

From the street I would look up, trying to figure out which window was hers. I had visions of flying into their house, swooping down, grabbing Rory off her bed and taking her to a safe distance above all the lunacy. If I really was a superhero I could've gotten Rory out of the house, caught the Son of Sam and somehow saved Mrs. Gallagher's life. I didn't even know what a .44-caliber revolver or a cancer cell looked like, but they were the same—two invisible monsters that snuck up on people and killed them. Surely Batman must have had some kind of weapon that could beat both of them. But, pretend as I did, I couldn't stop either one of them.

RORY HAD A kid sister named Kerri who was in my grade. To me, the most interesting thing about Kerri was that she had a sister named Rory. Kerri only waited a week to come back to school after her mother died and right off the bat there was an incident. I walked by her and accidentally bumped into her desk. Her crayon slipped out of the lines and she lost it.

"Look what you did! You ruined my picture! I'm sick of this! First my brothers and now you! I'm sick of it! Do you hear me? I'm sick of it!"

It was like I had accidentally knocked a knife off a table and didn't catch it for fear of getting cut. I jumped out of the way and let it fall. I had a feeling it wasn't about her picture, but I didn't know what else to do. Mrs. Johnson said, "OK, Kerri that's enough. Why don't you sit down now."

She didn't even wipe her nose or her eyes until a drop landed on her picture.

Outbursts weren't Kerri's only form of grieving. A few times she just got really quiet and said she wasn't feeling well. She'd go to the school nurse and her father got called at work to come pick her up. Mrs. Johnson explained to us that she thought Kerri wasn't sick, but rather she was upset about her mom. That I understood.

The thing that didn't make sense was the water fountain.

The class was silently staring into workbooks, trying to solve three-digit subtraction problems, when I went to get a drink. Bent over with my mouth near the faucet, I felt someone come up behind me. I turned around; it was Kerri. She was standing uncomfortably close but wasn't looking at me. She had her eyes on the fountain. I wiped my mouth and stepped around her cautiously, not sure if she was done throwing tantrums.

Two days later, same thing again. Got up right behind me, stood close and still didn't look at me.

I couldn't see why the girl who, weeks before, chewed me out in front of everyone now needed to stand so close and put her mouth to the same faucet right after mine.

The third time I wasn't even thirsty. I only wanted to see if it would happen again. By the time I had my face over the faucet, Kerri was behind me. Mrs. Johnson announced—so everyone could hear—how she'd noticed that every time Joseph got up for a drink, Kerri did also. When all the heads and giggles pointed in Kerri's direction, Mrs. Johnson asked if Kerri was really thirsty. Kerri answered her question by sitting down.

In the second grade, we didn't expect to have to deal with adults who couldn't see it was uncool to publicly embarrass a kid who lost her mother a month ago. Nor did we expect in the summer ahead of us there would be a citywide blackout, that Elvis Presley would die so young, that a bomb threat would evacuate thirty-five thousand people from the World Trade Center or that the Son of Sam would turn out to be a twenty-four-year-old guy named David who lived in our neighborhood a few blocks from where we played. How could we have conceptualized evil as a quiet guy who worked at the post office, rented the studio apartment down the street and lived among us? Fifteen years earlier he attended our elementary school, was taught by the same teachers, sat at our desks and drank out of the same water fountain. As grade school children, we had no idea that we were months away from those kinds of thoughts.

WE THOUGHT IT was him.

Kerri and I tried to play as if the water fountain incidents never happened. Catherine and I pushed our curfew. The sun was setting. We stopped the game for the car coming down the street. When it got close, we saw it was cream-colored, then we saw there was one guy in it.

Some kids took off and ran through front yards, between houses. Some screamed. I couldn't run. I fell backward, put my forearms in front of my face, not wanting to see or be seen. When I peeked out from behind my arms, he was halfway down the block; my sister was through our front door. It was time to run home, but not without my ball. I ran to Kerri, who was on the sidewalk, her whole body wrapped around the kickball.

I said, "Give me the ball," and tried to pry it from her. She rolled over and wouldn't let me grab it.

"Come on!" I said.

She wasn't giving it up. On top of her, I tried to get my hands between her stomach and the ball. She was fighting me. I rolled her on her back—she was laughing. Not a good time for a game of keep-away, I thought. I tried to punch the ball loose but never meant to knock the wind out of her. She held her ribs and cried. I said I was sorry, but she didn't even look back as she ran to her house. Someone had been yelling for her to get the hell inside. The screen door slammed behind her, then Rory appeared behind it. Her hair was gone, cut straggly, close to her head; it looked like she'd done it herself. She yelled at me, "Get out of here! Go home!"

My mother grabbed me by the back of my shirt and didn't let go until we were in our house. She yelled at me for not running home like my sister and wanted to know if I knew how to listen.

Nowhere. From now on, after dinner, we were to go nowhere.

I went into my room, closed the door and slammed the ball against my dresser; my lamp fell. I thought about the smile on Kerri's face while she wrestled me for the ball. Kerri Gallagher likes me? I grabbed the windowpane, tried to look up the block and only saw the streetlights come on.

Kerri Gallagher likes me.

THE NEXT MORNING we ate our cereal without talking as the radio played the news in the background. When it was time to go to school, we were handed our lunch boxes.

We stepped outside. It felt as if an overnight snowfall had covered the entire neighborhood in three feet of silence.

When we pulled up to school, Catherine and I leaned over the front seat to kiss our mom goodbye. She waited until we walked in the front door to drive away.

Kerri spoke to no one. During lunch hour she was sitting on a bench next to two other girls who were making finger puppets out of lined paper. I didn't have it in me to go over to her. Only when we were all making our way back into the school was I able to walk up next to her and ask if she was OK. She didn't even answer me.

We all sat at our desks and were told to get our math workbooks out.

I didn't want to do anything Mrs. Johnson said. It made no sense why she had embarrassed Kerri yesterday. It made no sense why the cops couldn't catch the .44-Caliber Killer or why parents yell at their children when they're trying to protect them or why we had to solve three-digit subtraction problems again.

While they all had their heads down, I went for the fountain. I drank, then turned back around. No one was standing close to me. Everyone still had their heads in their books. I went to the closet and poked through my lunch box. Mrs. Johnson asked me what I was doing. I told her I broke my pencil; I was just getting a new one. I opened my lunch box and took off the top of my thermos—the part that doubles as a cup. I went to the water fountain and filled it up. Walking toward Kerri, I was terrified that Mrs. Johnson was going to embarrass the hell out of me, too. I fought the urge to look to the front of the room to see if she was watching. Kerri was hunched over her desk, intent on her arithmetic. It happened so fast. I don't remember walking back to my desk. Kerri never looked up to see if anyone saw it. She only slid the cup closer to her with her left hand and kept writing with the other. She kept it near her like she was going to save it for when she really needed it. I never noticed it before, but when she leaned over like that her hair was long enough to reach her desk.

THE BIGGEST, MOST SILENT THING

I can't cook yet, she says.

I hang out in the kitchen because I like food and because my mother always asks me to keep her company. I'm eight; I know how to cook. Maybe it's an Italian thing. She turns the radio on to an oldies station and some guy is singing about taking his girl away into the moonlight, throwing her eyes into the sky, loving her in some deep moment of bliss forever and ever. Maybe it's a fifties thing. She says, now I can cook, rubs her palms together and grabs me by the waist. Let me show you how we used to dance when I was a kid. You put your hands here like you're leading, 'cause that's how the guys did it, but really you're gonna follow. Just follow me. You just kind of rock back and forth, that's right. She sings along and hums when she can't remember the words. She says, you know what I want for Christmas this year? I want a special gift. What? I ask. I want you to write a poem about me. A poem just about me. Then she says, oops, we can't let this burn. She reaches to the stove and pushes the escarole around in the pan, her right hand still around my waist.

THE NEXT NIGHT, my mother asks me to go with her to pick up my sister from religious instruction class. I say it's too early to go and she says she wants to drive slowly because the roads may be icy. On our way out the door we run into our neighbor Gloria, and my mother asks her if she had a nice Thanksgiving. Gloria went to her sister's in Philadelphia and, she says, she'll be going there for Christmas as well. My mother says, that's nice. Three years ago, Gloria's husband took off without notice and wrote her a letter explaining where he was and who he was with and served her with papers two weeks later. I am quiet. She says, hi, Joey. Hi, Gloria. Mom tells Gloria to stop by if she needs anything.

Mom says, give me your arm, Joey, there's ice on these steps. They need salt on them. I told your stepfather to do it, she says, but who knows with him. She asks me if I'll put some salt down when we get back and I say, yes. As we walk down the stairs, she sticks to my arm and tells me how sorry she feels for Gloria being alone during the holidays. I can relate to her very well, she says. Of course I can. She's had two last names and I've already had three.

During the drive, she asks me if I'm excited to go to my father's house for Christmas Eve. I say, yeah, and she wants to know what Patty, my stepmother, cooks for Christmas Eve dinner. I say, fish and things. Is it good? she wants to know. I say it is.

We pull up to the Catholic school twenty minutes early. We sit quietly in the car. My breath turns to vapor out the window. Mom tells me she's cold and can I roll the window up a little. I leave it open a crack. She says the church looks like the one in the Bronx she and my father went to when they were still married. And that was the beginning of the history lesson. It dated back before I was born, when Mom and Dad weren't having a good time. When, my mother tells me, my father wasn't always nice. When he wasn't nice to her. She tells me how he used to yell at her and hit her and how he started dating Patty while they were still married. I always figured it was that way. There had been many innuendos and opinions thrown around the house that weren't intended to land in my ears. This is the first formal sit-down on the subject. I feel like the kid in class who's terrified to get called on. I just take notes, ask no questions and try to be invisible.

When the history lesson is over, she brings us in to the present by talking about my last report card. It left a lot to be desired, she says. The kids start coming out of the Catholic school and Mom says we'll talk more about it later. She starts up the car and I can see my sister Catherine walking toward us. I think maybe we can talk about the apostles on the ride home. My mother says, Joey, can you roll up that window, please, Mommy's cold.

Later, I get the talk about the report card. My mother has trouble understanding why my sister does so well in school and I don't. The thing is, it doesn't occur to me to be a good student when my sister already is. That's her calling. Why should I do that? There's no reason for two people in one family to play the same part.

My mother tells me that no one is going to come along and just give me good grades. Or give me anything else, for that matter. She wants to know how I think the family eats around here and how I get clothes to wear. She says, what do you want to do when you get older? I tell her I want to be a baseball player. And what if that doesn't work out? she says. Then what? What are you going to do then? I say, I don't know. She says I have to know because life isn't a game. I say, I don't know, OK? I don't know what I want. Then she explodes. Don't say that. It just kills me that you could say that. She looks like she's going to spit. You sound just like your father.

I GO OUTSIDE to throw salt on the front steps. I see Gloria's TV on and I watch my breath turn to steam again. I wrote a poem once, when I was six. In the first grade I went on a school trip to the Museum of Natural History. The intention for most of the first-graders (at least all the boys) was to see how much trouble they could cause. But something in me didn't want to. The museum didn't feel like the kind of place where we should've been causing trouble. I thought, *Don't fuck around. See if you can learn something.* Go somewhere and learn something. It was the first time a thought like that had ever occurred to me. So I went to the butterfly exhibit and learned how they camouflage themselves. They hold the top part of their wings—the bright, colorful side—together so only the underside of the wings shows. The underside is covered with browns and grays, which allow them to blend in with dirt and branches. They become invisible in their own surroundings. They hide their beauty for safety. This is known as crypsis. I took a Magic Marker and wrote "crypsis" on my arm and covered it with my sleeve.

Then I saw the blue whale they have on the ceiling. It was the biggest and most silent thing I'd seen. All the other big stuff I knew was so damn loud—our house, the school, my parents' divorce, dinner. Even my mother's new marriage was loud. My stepfather was a very low-key individual. The longest conversation I ever had with him went like this: What time's the Yankee game on? Seven o'clock. When my mother would fight him, he would never fight back, so she would have to fight herself. She'd lock herself in the bathroom, yelling at my stepfather through the door. She'd scream about the life he had promised her and how good things were supposed to have been and how it was all bullshit. That's how she fought him. He never screamed back. The loudest thing I ever heard my stepfather say to my mother was, "No, I'm not like your ex-husband. I don't beat you."

That was really loud.

So I wrote a poem about the blue whale on the ceiling at the Museum of Natural History. The poem said that the biggest thing I ever saw was also the quietest. Mom hung it on the refrigerator. Also, I took my blue Magic Marker and I drew a picture of the whale on the bottom of my kitchen chair. Then I would lie on the floor and look up at my picture, so the whale could be over my head, just like they had it at the museum. Also, no one else would see it there.

When I come back in the house, the report card discussion continues. She says, Joseph, I know you're a smart kid. I know you can do very good in school, that's the only reason why I get upset, OK? She throws a hug on me and my head lands in her stomach. She plays with my hair and asks me if I've locked the side door. I say I have. See, she says, and holds me tighter, poor Gloria, she doesn't have a man around the house anymore. It's scary. God forbid someone tries to break into her house at night, what's she gonna do?

LIKE EVERY SATURDAY morning, our father comes to pick my sister and me up at our mother's house and then we stay with him for the weekend. I sit in the back and my sister in the front. He drives a Volkswagen Bug and the gears are tight, which makes for a jerky ride every time he shifts. It's not something that's happened to me before. I've never peed my pants in my mother's car. But I feel it rising up now as soon as I get into his car. This Saturday morning, I get a tender feeling below my stomach when we stop at the light. It gets worse when he starts to drive, then he throws it into second, the car jerks and it happens. My sister notices first and says, Daddy, Joey needs help.

My father looks at me in the rearview mirror and says, what's the matter, Joey? You OK?

When he realizes what's happened, he stops the car, gets a towel out from under the hood and spreads it out on the seat next to me. He says, Joey, it's OK. You're not hurt. It's OK, Joey. Sit on this now and we'll put on different clothes when we get home. That's all. It's OK.

When we get back to his place, my stepmother cleans me up. I wear my pajama bottoms while I wait for my jeans to dry. I walk out of the bathroom to the living room, where Dad's sitting in an armchair.

Come here. Sit with me, Joey. Sit with your old man.

He lifts me up. My father has hands that feel solid as two pieces of teak furniture. My butt lands on one arm of the chair and my feet on the other. He goes, sit here on the big chair like a man. There we go. You feel better?

Yeah, I say.

See, no big deal. He drags his thumb across my neck. It feels as big as the barrel end of a baseball bat. What happened to your neck? he wants to know. You wrestling with someone?

No.

Then who grabbed you?

I say, someone in class. I was hoping he would drop it there.

Who? he asks.

Kerri.

Kerri? Oh, yeah? This, he is very interested in. Kerri who?

Gallagher.

Huh. An Irish girl. Is she nice?

Yeah.

He says, you like her? I smile. He pokes me in the ribs with a finger. I'm sure she's very nice. She cute?

I think I'm not supposed to tell my dad how cute I think girls are. So I keep it shut and hope he puts this subject to sleep.

Aaaah, Joey, he says. Girls . . . they're different than guys. If only women understood that, less marriages would go into retirement. Patty, she understands. I'll tell you something, it's like this—you like this girl Kerri, and maybe there's another girl that you like also. Right?

Um . . . no.

No? No one? I shake my head. Well, someday there will be. And you'll find yourself trying to understand why you like them both, you'll start to feel a lot of things and you'll get confused, but let me tell you, it's simple. There are some things that guys need that ladies do not. And this is the whole difference between them. A guy needs the kind of thing he can keep his feelings out of. And this is the thing that your stepmother understands what many women—I don't mention names—don't understand, and that is why a lot of marriages go south. You know what I mean?

He continued.

Look, a guy needs the kind of thing that he can keep his feelings out of. And I don't think women can do that, they're too emotional. A woman can't fall down an elevator shaft, for instance, dust herself off, then have sex with you ten seconds later. If they don't feel it, it's not gonna happen. Period. But *guys* can get into a *plane wreck* and *lose limbs*. Two hundred fifty dead bodies floating in the ocean, sharks are eating the survivors and in the life raft as the helicopters are coming, the guy will hit on the stewardess. And this is true. Some women don't understand how we could do a thing at a time like that. If the stewardess is hot, then we can do it. It's simple. So what, she may have lost a limb. We'd still do it. Even in the face of death. They think we're just pigs. Let 'em do their claptrappin'. I'll tell you the truth, son, we're not *pigs,* we're just *different.*

The only thing I'm sure of is that his lips are moving and sound is coming out of them. Sharks? Helicopters? Pigs with no arms? He could be conjugating Cantonese verbs into Sanskrit, for all I know.

He goes on.

And this is what Patty understands that many women do not. She doesn't judge. And who should? Who should be able to judge a thing like that? It's not the kind of thing . . . Your Grandfather used to say, "He who casts the first stone who lives in glass houses . . . you shouldn't do it." Your stepmother understands that we're different. You understand, Joey?

What if you like only one girl? I ask. Then what?

Then that's OK. It's OK if you like only one girl for now. I mean, you'll see. There will be plenty, is all I'm saying. Someday you'll have your own place, you'll have your own stuff . . .

My father gets introspective. It's unfamiliar to me. When he comes out of it, it's hard for him to look me in the eye. He speaks slower and deeper than he has been. Joey, he says, when you get older—sometimes I think, probably, you might think of me and you'll say, "You know, my dad was a real jerk-off when it came to certain things, but then other things he was OK with." I hope.

Now he tries to lighten himself up.

Don't tell your mother this, he says, but secretly I can't wait for you to get older so we can get dressed up and go out—you're gonna look sharp. Always look sharp, Joey. It's important. You see, my father, your grandpa . . . he used to go out alone. And I think we can do better than that.

There is a heavy pause.

We all work with what we have, he says.

Another one.

You know how to listen, Joey. It's a good thing to know how to do.

He grabs my arm and pulls at what little muscle is there and says, Jesus, look at you. When did you get so big?

I try to figure out how to break away from those hands. It seems he wants to be friends, something I think parents aren't supposed to be. I understand the way dogs feel when they want to walk one way and their leash is getting pulled the other.

I say, I'm hungry. Can we have lunch now?

Sure we can. He calls to the kitchen, Patty, can you fix the kids something?

She says, I got ham sandwiches.

He says to me, you like that, right?

Happy to have a destination, I say, I love ham.

He kisses me on the top of my head, lifts me off the chair and as I head for the kitchen, one of his palms catches me square on the ass.

THERE'S A RUNNING joke in my mother's house. For years, she's been talking about this mink coat she's gonna buy herself. We say, "How's the mink coat fund comin', Ma? You save enough to buy the claws yet?" She says, "Yeah, you watch. The day I get that coat I'm gonna be laughin' hard. You watch." She works nights at a department store and her husband delivers bread. Where does a mink coat fit into that picture?

But this night, December 17, 1979, she calls us on our joke. We've just finished dinner. My sister, my mother, my stepfather and myself linger over empty dishes and I pick olives out of the salad with my fingers. Our mother says she has an announcement to make. Announcement? My sister and I make faces and validate each other's confusion. We hardly ever have anything to talk about in this house. Who makes announcements?

Mom says, I bought myself a Christmas present this year and it was ready a little early, so I thought I would show it to all of you. Wait here.

My sister presses our stepfather for what it is while our mother runs upstairs. He says he has no idea and it seems as if he's coming clean. Even if he wasn't, that was OK, because my sister and I had a secret on him.

Not too long ago my sister and I were in the kitchen with our mom and she told us about that night at work. Some guy came in the store and was looking for this perfume for his mother and asked our mom if she would tell him where to find it. Sure, she said, follow me. The guy said that he'd follow our mother anywhere. After the guy bought the perfume, he told our mom about the boat he owned and how he would love to take her out on it sometime. You made my week, my month, my year, our mom said to the guy. But I don't think the boat would be big enough for the rest of my family. So he left, she said.

We hear Mom coming back down the stairs, then she appears in the kitchen. Our jaws drop, our eyes blink. She's wearing a silver and gray mink jacket. It is the first time Catherine and I are allowed to say *holy shit* and not get yelled at. But when our stepfather says the same thing, Mom hits him in the arm and says, watch your mouth.

Catherine and I jump her like two kittens on a scratching post. We fall off and then claw our way back up. She's never felt softer and never seemed so excited.

She opens it up to show us the inside.

What does it have embroidered in it? This thing that she wanted so badly and fed a nickel-and-dime savings for over eight years? What is stitched in the inside of it? Margaret Anne. Her first name and her middle name.

Catherine says, Margaret Anne. Why doesn't it say your last name?

Mom holds the fluffy collar up to her face and snuggles in it. That's all I wanted it to say.

Our stepfather, her husband, says nothing.

ONCE, WHEN SOME of the shingles on our roof came loose, my mother asked my stepfather to fix them. Getting up to the roof was easy, but on his way down, my stepfather got stuck and yelled to my mother and me. We came running out of the kitchen to see him lying on his stomach with his arms spread out, trying to hug the roof. He was reaching with his feet, trying to find the ladder under him. He asked if any of the neighbors were around to help him. His voice was tight. My mother said, "Joey, go help your stepfather." I climbed up the ladder to the roof and said to him, "Your foot is almost on the ladder, just slide down a little more. Now you're about six inches away from it. All you have to do is keep moving your foot down and you'll feel the step."

That conversation my stepfather and I had a few years ago, the one about what time the Yankee game was on, moved into the position of second longest.

He found the ladder with his foot, climbed down and I stayed up on the roof for a little while longer. I had never seen the neighborhood from that perspective.

THAT NIGHT, AFTER the mink jacket goes back to the closet, my mother, my stepfather and I sit in front of the TV. Mom says,

Joey, bring me a blanket, please. My stepfather's head bobs back and forth until my mother cuts in. She says his name. He doesn't hear. She says it louder and he jumps awake. What? She says, why don't you go to sleep?

I'm just gonna stay up a little longer.

You're already asleep, go to bed.

He does.

She says, come sit on the couch with Mommy. I do. The TV throws blue patterns on the wall. I wonder how this Friday night ritual got started. She takes her glasses off and rubs her eyes and asks if I've locked the side door. I have. She throws some of her blanket over my legs. Eventually her eyes flicker and her head falls back.

THE NEXT DAY. My clothes are all packed for the weekend at my dad's. I go to my stepfather, who is alone reading the paper. I'm still not sure how to strike up a conversation with him, let alone ask him for help. I approach him as if I have a secret. I say, I know what Mommy wants for Christmas.

He says, what? playing along with the secret, and looks up.

She wants someone to write a poem for her.

A poem?

Yeah, I say. A real one. I was hinting.

He goes, wow.

Hint not taken. I say, you can do that, right?

Well, Joey. I don't know. Did she say what it should be about? About her.

That's a tough one, Joey.

I know.

Well . . . It takes him a long time to talk again. Did she say it could be funny?

This could be good, maybe he's already thinking of content.

I say, she didn't say if it could be funny or not, so I guess it could be.

About the past or the present?

Whatever, I guess.

Now he is quiet. I'm hoping he'll say, no problem, then I'll say thank you and leave.

I don't think that's something I can do. But you can write it, Joe.

I think, *No fuckin' way,* but I say, why can't you?

I'm not much of a writer, he says. And I already got her a present.

This sucks. This is now our longest conversation in history, but it's not our smoothest. So he already bought her a present. It doesn't matter. I know that whatever he bought her, she'll open it up say, "Oh, how beautiful," hold it up for everyone to see, thank him, kiss him on his cheek and wonder where the poem is.

Also, Joey, if she asked you to do it, then that means she wants you to do it. He tells me, in a very encouraging tone, that I have a week.

What if it's no good? I say.

All presents are good.

But what if she doesn't like it? We can't return it.

He laughs at this, then says, you can only give what you can, Joey.

What I don't say is that I simply don't want to do it. What I don't ask is how I became in charge of writing the love poems around the house. And how I became in charge of salting the stairs, putting my mother to bed, stirring the sauce so it didn't stick and locking the doors.

Weakly, I say, but that's what Mommy wants.

Joey, when people don't get everything they ask for, sometimes they blame other people for it. And really it's no one's fault. He tries to see if this has landed on me. You don't always get what you want for Christmas, do you?

No.

And you're not mad, right?

No.

Mom walks in and says, Joey, your father's here. Didn't you hear the horn? Catherine is already out there. Come say goodbye.

CATHERINE AND I get into our father's car and we start to drive. The car is jerking around. Our dad asks if we're excited about Christmas. My sister asks if Patty's going to make stuffed clams like last year. I try to hold myself off the seat with my arms when I feel tender in the bladder area. The car jerks away as the light changes. My father wants to know if we would like pizza for lunch. Catherine looks back at me; she knows what has already happened.

She says, Dad, Joey needs help.

Brian was so small I could carry him on one shoulder. He'd perch up there; I'd wrap my arm around his shins for balance. In fourth, fifth and sixth grade, this was our favorite means of transportation. I did a lot of growing in those years. Much more than he did. (The hems on my jeans, bought in September, had to be let out by March. He wore holes through the knees before his hems needed to be dropped.) To this day, my right shoulder hangs three-quarters of an inch lower than my left. Whatever you carry around as a kid reserves the right and the power to mold you, even years after you put it down.

I brought home the class pictures from fifth grade. The smallest kids were sitting in the front. I was standing up in the back row, looking like a sailor on a three-day pass. My mother looked at the picture and said, "Look at you, slouched over like that. Why don't you stand up straight?" I can understand why she thought I looked uneven. Because between my head and my right shoulder, all she saw was empty space.

FEEL YOUR FEET on the infield. This is the first part of your job. Because then, when someone hits a hard line drive down the third base line, and the energy of the ball tells you where to go, you can take two side steps, push off this infield and dive with an outstretched arm. There's no deciding time (the decisions are built into the organizing principles of the game—you must get your body to the ball), there's only reacting time. If this ball connects with your mitt, its energy will stop dead. That's when you'll experience the mitt as an extension of your body. If you get the ball to the first baseman before the runner gets there, you got the job done. You've connected with whatever was hurled in your direction and passed it on to the only person who could do anything further with it.

The same principle applies to batting. Connect with whatever comes into the strike zone. To accomplish this—many say—is one of the most difficult things in all of sports. The amount of time it takes a batter to swing is about equal to the time it takes for the ball to travel from the pitcher's hand to the catcher's mitt, thus leaving the batter minimal time to discern whether or not the pitch is worthy of a swing. The average success rate for the average batter to connect with a pitch is one in twenty-five. Unless the batter was myself, when I was eight years old, and had a batting average of .856. It was hard for me to miss; what can I tell you? Hitting for me was like unlocking your door while you're sorting through your mail. Next thing you know, you're in. You thought nothing of the dexterity it took. A developed skill felt like an instinct.

But I won't send you to the brink with stories of my illustrious Little League career. Because skill is never what it's all about anyway. Luck can beat skill any given day.

WHEN I WAS little, I was convinced I was going to grow up and play for the New York Yankees. That was all it seemed I needed to do. It was the thing that could ward off a life of loserhood and failure, and deliver me to heroism. As a kid, being a fan of the New York Yankees meant being surrounded by magic. Only the

Yankees had the players who could hit three home runs off three consecutive pitches in a single World Series game. Between the ages of five and ten I saw the Yankees play four World Series. No other team in the history of any sport has won more world championships. When the Yankees weren't televised I'd listen to the broadcast on the little transistor radio we had. I'd go to the garage roof, where I could get the best reception, and listen to Phil Rizzuto, Frank Messer or Bill White commentate on the game and my future.

At ten years old, I was one of the best players around. Whenever I went to Yankee Stadium, I knew. At the stadium there are small tunnels that lead from the enclosure of the concession stands and bathrooms to the grandstands. The moment I walked through the tunnel and the sight of the field and the sound of the crowd opened up, I knew it was only a matter of time before I would be on the field. I couldn't imagine a better way to spend a life.

By the time I was fourteen, though, better players started to strike me out, hit home runs off me, even pick me off first base. It's hard to pinpoint the moment when I realized my future wasn't going to play out according to the specifications of my dreams. Sometime before I played the game in which I intentionally hit Brian, I already knew.

BRIAN FREIDMAN WAS the smartest, wittiest kid around, and by sixth grade had everybody by the balls with his charm. In school, he charmed his way so far over the student/teacher line that it ceased to exist. Brian laughed at people when they carried on as if there were delineation between student and teacher, father and son, husband and wife. To him, it was all the same. Anything you gave him, he'd give right back. If you were afraid to ask something, he'd go ahead and tell you. Everything was in fair territory.

Our sixth-grade class was in the computer room with Mr. Kleinrock. We were all sitting at a huge rectangular table. Brian sat between me and a girl named Kerri Gallagher. Kerri dropped her pen under the table and crawled underneath to get it. Mr. Kleinrock came over and said, "Brian, where's Kerri?"

"She's under the table," Brian said.

"What's she doing under the table?"

Without looking up from his computer screen, Brian said, "Givin' head?"

Although Mr. Kleinrock didn't want to, he laughed like the rest of us.

And then there was the day in seventh grade when a kid named Danny Ryan came to school crying. It was the same day that, in an unrelated incident, Brian pissed off our English teacher, Mrs. Bochnack.

In the library, Brian, this kid John Nolan and I sat at a round table while Mrs. Bochnack scolded Brian. John was Danny's next-door neighbor, so he had all the information about Danny. Mrs. Bochnack was in Brian's face telling him what it meant to show respect. During her tirade, I leaned over to John and said, "What's the matter with Danny? Why's he crying?"

John said, "His dog died."

"How?" I asked.

In the middle of receiving his scolding, without taking his eyes off the teacher or losing the hyper-serious look on his face, under his breath Brian answered for John. "Car accident."

John and I laughed, and when we realized Mrs. Bochnack was too involved in her tirade to notice Brian had ever spoken, we knew this situation had beautiful potential.

"What kind of dog was it?" I asked John.

Brian held his hands out in front of him, palms one foot apart, facing each other. And out of the corner of his mouth, he said, "Little Pekingese, about this big."

Teacher didn't notice that one, either, just kept yelling at Brian. Now it was officially a game.

"Did they see who hit it?" I asked

"Nope," said Brian. Still staring into the teacher's eyes.

"Is Danny upset?"

Brian said, "Very."

John couldn't hold back the laughs.

"Are they gonna get another dog?" I asked.

Then Brian screamed and made like he was slamming his head on the desk. "I don't want another dog! It's not gonna be the same! I want Buddy!"

All Mrs. Bochnack could do was walk away and admit that she didn't have what it took.

SO MANY DAYS from the third grade to the sixth, I'd go over to Brian's house after school. His father wouldn't come home until six, and his mother would be asleep on the couch; she worked nights. Didn't matter how quiet we were when we walked in: Her son was coming home, she instinctively woke up. When he was in an affectionate mood, Brian would go to the couch and fix the covers that his mom had twisted up in her sleep. He'd pull them up to her neck, tuck them beneath the cushions, maybe kiss her.

I got to be an honorary member of the Freidman house. Meaning, I didn't have to ring the doorbell before coming in, or ask before I went into the refrigerator. However, if we went to my house after school we didn't spend so much time inside because everyone was always home and awake. At the Friedmans', though, we'd always head right to the kitchen and make ice cream floats.

We played our positions well. I'd get the glasses, because Brian couldn't reach them without climbing on the counter, and that's a lot of noise. He'd get the ice cream from the freezer and the soda from the refrigerator and all things landed on the table in unison. Then I went to one drawer for spoons and he to another drawer for the ice cream scoop. Back to the table, where I'd pour just the right amount of soda in each glass. This is a crucial step. If you don't pour enough, the ice cream hits the insufficient amount of soda and you wind up with a glass full of milky bubbles. If you pour too much, you're headed for an overflow. You can try to dissolve the bubbles with a spoon or sip the overflow with a straw, but neither method ever works. It gets to the point where you'll just have to admit you're ruined—that the operation has to shut down. Even if you can muster the courage to start again, your momentum has been wiped out of your dessert-making. This happened to Brian and me maybe once every three months.

BASEBALL WAS NEVER really Brian's sport. He held the bat with the awkwardness of someone trying to blow his first note out of a slide trombone, unsure where his hands were supposed to go and unable to get a nice sound out of it. When the pitches came by, he'd counter them with brassy-hollow misses. He was always batting eighth or ninth and playing the outfield. We played in the same Little League organization from ages eight through fourteen. So we spent much of our time on baseball fields, in and out of uniform. Sometimes, after school, we'd walk around the neighborhood and wind up on a baseball field. This was where we'd talk about girls, find empty nickel bags, remnants of joints, used condoms that we might have touched with a stick. This was where we talked about things, it seemed, other people couldn't understand. If it was a Friday night and we could stay out late, we would lay down in the outfield and watch the sunset turn into stars. It was a whole different place without a crowd, uniforms and an umpire.

Brian once told me that he asked his dad if he always wanted to be a mailman. His dad said, "No." When Brian asked him why he did it his father said, "If you want to have a family and a place to put them and things for them to eat, you have to do something. I make good money at my job." Then Brian asked him why he didn't find a job he loved. His dad said, "If you wait too long, you wind up falling through the cracks. So you gotta grab the opportunities that come at you."

———

IN THE FOURTH grade, my sister and my mother were driving me to baseball practice.

"Hold on!" My sister reached from the back seat to the dashboard and turned the radio up. "I think this is it. Everybody be quiet."

With her hand on the knob, she listened to the music as if tomorrow's winning lottery numbers were being revealed. A man sang over keyboards, guitars and a drum. His voice was almost subdued, waiting, it seemed, for the right time to explode into a celebration that would end loneliness forever.

"This is it!" she screamed. "This is the guy I was telling you about! Holy shit, this is it!"

"Watch your mouth," my mother said with borderline resignation.

My sister turned it up louder. Now the speakers in my mom's 1974 Dart Swinger cracked and distorted the music, but my ears were pinned.

My sister had heard it, his third album, a few weeks before. A kid named Steven Cantor was playing it the day the seventh-graders went on an end-of-the-year picnic. She came home that night and said, "Joey, you gotta hear this guy I heard. It's incredible. I can't describe it; you just gotta hear it."

The part of the song I remember most is when it crescendos, he counts to four, then screams about how the highway is jammed with broken heroes, and about how everybody is running tonight, but there's no place left to hide. It was the best thing I ever heard—beyond the sound of a raucous grandstand or a long fly ball slapping against a leather glove. I didn't know anything about music. I didn't know how to hold a guitar, play a piano or read music. But when I heard Bruce Springsteen count to four and sing that line, I knew what I was going to do. *That.* That thing that he just did. I didn't know in what way, but that's what I wanted to do. I never told anybody about that.

And another thing I never mentioned to anyone happened one Saturday night, while I was staying at my father's apartment. I couldn't sleep. I lay in bed, my face to his bookshelf, reading the titles sideways. This was something I did often when I couldn't sleep in my father's apartment. It got to the point that I knew almost every title on the shelf by heart. The one book I was most curious about was my father's high school yearbook. This was the night I finally took it off the shelf.

He walked in just as I started leafing through it. "What's the matter, Joey?"

"Can't sleep."

"Whaddaya got there?"

"Um, this is your yearbook."

"Oh."

I wasn't sure where he stood on me looking through it. He sat down next to me, took the book and put himself in charge of turning the pages. I caught flashes of guys' heads and pictures of what the Bronx looked like back then.

"You went to an all-boys school?"

"Yup."

He stopped on one page and pointed to a picture. "Jesus, Tony Gallucci. See this guy? I saw this guy eat a gypsy-moth caterpillar."

"Eew. Why'd he do that?"

"He was crazy. And someone gave him a dollar."

He turned the page. "And this guy, Patsy Muzz. His last name was really Mussolini. Me and Patsy ate thirteen hot dogs once. At Carmine's Hot Dogs on the corner of Baychester Avenue an' two-thirty-thirty. Right near the projects. Carmine had the best hot dogs with onions I ever ate."

I said, "I can't even eat seven hot dogs."

"We didn't eat *seven,* we ate *thirteen.*"

"Each? Thirteen hot dogs each?"

"Yeah. You kiddin'?"

"How do you do that?"

"First you eat one, then you eat another one, and you keep goin' until you get to thirteen." He kept flipping the pages. "Mike Segusso. Mikey Goosey, we called him. Billy Sotto. We called him Billy Buckwheat because he was the only Puerto Rican guy in our group. Although the real Buckwheat was black. Anyway . . . oh, look at this guy. Look at his glasses. Look how thick they are. Joey Binocs, we called him. Joey was a good stickball player. He used to hit the ball so high, we called them altitudials. Jesus, this feels like a hundred years ago."

Under the pictures of these guys was a list of the activities or sports they were involved in, or any academic awards they might have received. Then, under that, each guy wrote the occupation he wished to pursue in the future. But some guys had nothing at all written under their pictures. I pointed to one of these guys. "Dad, why doesn't he have anything under his name?"

"Because he never was anything and never wanted to be anything."

My father searched the page for a moment longer, then said, "That's enough." He closed the book and put it on the shelf. "You think you'll be able to sleep all right?"

"Yeah. I'm OK."

He kissed me on the head and went back to his bedroom. I waited to hear his door shut, got out of bed, picked up the yearbook and turned to his picture. *I never knew that,* I thought. Underneath his photograph there was no list of school activities. Just one word: Actor.

BRIAN AND I would not go to high school together.

The idea itself went against all laws of logic. My last name was Frascone, his was Freidman. Those spellings would secure us a place right next to each other in homeroom for the next four years. But things were happening in the place where we grew up that annulled even the promise of our names.

In the early 1980s, a group of lawyers who represented the NAACP brought a case against the Board of Education, City of Yonkers, claiming that the city was segregating its schools. Our mayor decided to make their case a little easier on them by offering a "consent decree." Meaning, he would back the judge in whatever his decision was and never motion for the case to go to the Supreme Court. So it never did. These NAACP lawyers (who had children in private schools and "shitloads of money," as my family never tired of pointing out) won their case.

A desegregation program was issued that not only had to do with trying to balance the schools, but the whole city. The west and south side of Yonkers was mostly black and Hispanic, while the north and east were predominately white. To desegregate the city, "affordable housing" was to be built in the "desirable" neighborhoods. In Yonkers, families who already lived in the "desirable" neighborhoods were largely working-class people who recently moved up from the outer boroughs of New York, from other "undesirable" neighborhoods in Queens, Brooklyn or the Bronx. These people were pissed off because they'd worked hard to get into a "desirable" place and now the city was bringing the "undesirable" neighborhood right back to them. Of course, this made people who lived in the "undesirable" neighborhoods feel unwelcome before they even moved into this "affordable housing." Needless to say, this court decision did wonders for racial tension and made real estate values drop at a ridiculous rate. No one would buy a house in Yonkers, and even if they'd wanted to, no one could afford to sell a house at the going rates.

It wasn't long before the city started to make a harsh rasping sound, caused by the rubbing together of seemingly different groups of people. This was all done in the name of promoting excellence and education in the Yonkers schools.

Because we were young teens, real estate values were not the first things on our mind. We didn't realize what racial tension could do. When the classes and the races tried to coexist, it seemed to leave us with two choices: to be the oppressed or to be the oppressor. It was hard for us to see other options and no one wanted to get caught on either side of that line.

By the time he was in eighth grade, Brian's parents decided to move an hour north of Yonkers. They sold their old house at a huge loss but didn't even care. They just wanted to run.

THE WORST THING Brian and I ever saw on the baseball field happened the summer before he left town. We were hanging out one day after Little League practice, watching a group of high school guys playing the game. A group of girls watched, too. After a few innings, Brian and I joined in. They let me play because I was good enough and they let Brian play because they needed another player.

Who knows how this shit starts. It doesn't take much.

All of a sudden, there was a small crowd surrounding two guys. One of the guys was holding a baseball bat and the other was not backing down. I didn't know these guys well, but I knew of them. Nicky Figueroa and Rob Caldera. Rob was a good five inches taller and twenty-five pounds heavier than Nicky. But Nicky held the bat. It wasn't a screaming match. For a moment they seemed to be composed and grounded, contented to be there. We'd all seen that before. Two guys circling each other, deciding if they were actually going to do it, trying to justify an attack. Or they might have been trying to get up enough anger so they could forget about justification and fight. Sometimes that took a while. But sometimes guys in a situation like this would just talk a lot of shit, finally walk away and the fight would never happen. So that's what the crowd was thinking—maybe this one might not happen.

And that's when it did happen. That's when Nicky caught Rob in the head with the bat. It sounded like someone punched a blackboard. The rigid body that Rob was using to stand up to Nicky went limp. His eyes went white and he fell on the dirt of the infield. It took a second for us to understand what had just happened. Nobody moved yet. Then Nicky did something I'd only ever expected to see in a movie. Rob was on the ground, clearly not moving, and Nicky, like he was swinging a golf club, hit Rob in the head once more. That was a different sound. That was the sound of someone's skull breaking. People jumped away as if someone had just dropped a live hand grenade. I saw a girl cover her eyes. Rob's blood got on peoples' sneakers.

It was over in less than ten seconds. Some people were too dazed to do anything about it. They just stood there feeling an unfamiliar motion in their stomachs. Finally, two guys got Nicky down to the ground and wrestled the bat away from him. Someone was yelling, "Call the fuckin' cops! Someone call the fuckin' cops!"

After the cops took statements and the ambulance drove off, Brian and I walked home together. We were mostly silent until I asked him what the name of his new high school was.

He said, "I don't know."

"You gonna play baseball?" I asked.

"Why would I?" He didn't really wait for an answer. "You?"

"No."

IT WAS THE last game of the season. And as far as the Little League standings went, not a very important one. Neither my team nor Brian's was going to make it to the playoffs, so no matter what, the season would end there. As would my baseball career.

I pitched and batted third in the lineup. Brian was in the outfield and batted eighth. In the bottom of the sixth, the score was tied. With one out and bases loaded, I struck out the number-seven batter, and—with two outs—Brian was now up.

He got into his stance, I set myself, we caught each other's eye and both of us had to hold back a laugh over the ridiculousness of a rivalry between us. My coach yelled, "Focus, Frascone. Easy out here. Easy out." The lack of enthusiasm coming off Brian's team's bench seemed to say they agreed.

With the ball in hand, staring into the target of the catcher's mitt, I wondered what it would say under my high school picture. Baseball was officially out. So what did I want to be? The crescendo in a Bruce Springsteen song? How do you do that? And what was Brian going to be? What it would say under his picture?

Here, I made my decision.

I threw a slow ball right over the middle of the plate. He swung and missed for strike one, but my coach was pissed. "Frascone! You're not gonna bring us out of the inning at that speed! Heat! I wanna see heat!"

Brian was still holding a smile as he took his stance. The next pitch was so slow it almost had an arc. Again, Brian swung and missed. I thought, *Do I have to go over there and hit this ball myself?*

My coach called a time-out and visited me on the mound.

"You OK?" he said.

"Yeah."

"Why you throwin' off-speed pitches?"

"I got him with it."

"You got lucky. We go into extra innings, we got the top of our lineup batting, this game is ours. Listen, this guy's not a hitter. Blow one past him and get us outta the inning. I wanna end this season with a win. OK?"

"OK."

I set myself on the mound. I thought, *He's small, but this shouldn't hurt too much.* I wound up, and with a precision fastball, hit Brian in his left arm.

He dropped his bat and trotted down the line. His team charged the field as their winning run crossed the plate. Brian threw me a quick smile as he leaped for first base and landed on it with both feet. His teammates were running after him.

My catcher was standing there crestfallen, the mask dangling from his hand. My coach and the rest of my team were silent. When I looked back at the crowd near first base, everyone was jumping on my friend. Brian had disappeared behind a team of screaming fourteen-year-olds.

I f she left a candle in the back window, that meant it was cool. Her older brother and her parents were asleep and the side door to the basement would be unlocked. That winter, before I'd sneak inside, I'd keep my hands against the heat vents of my car for a few minutes. Mostly she would be sleeping and wouldn't wake up until my hands were under her blankets. We would go right to the floor so the bed wouldn't make noise. If we spoke at all, our mouths were right against each other's ears. She used to sleep in the bedroom upstairs, where the rest of her family still slept, but a while earlier she moved to the room downstairs, away from them. We would mime our goodbye by the basement door. She'd be wrapped in a blanket. She'd put two fingers to her lips and then to mine. She'd put a lock of her hair in her mouth as I cautiously shut the door.

I GET OFF the phone, try to leave the house without my mother seeing I've been crying. From the living room she yells to ask how Roseanna is doing out there. I say, really good, then I leave. I get to the restaurant, where my friend Benny is the bar back. He tries to make me laugh, hooks me up with a free drink and asks what's eating me. I say I'm fine and he tells me I should maybe let her go. I say it's not about that, plus I have no choice, she's already gone. Then he says, maybe you should let go of her. I say, it's not about that. He says he hasn't known me that long but has never seen me look as if I could hurt myself. I should correct him if he's wrong, he adds. I don't correct him, nor do I offer further explanation.

I'm half juiced after a few. Benny wants to hug me over the bar but looks in my face and thinks better of it. I leave.

In the parking lot, I hear this guy and this girl fighting from inside a car. He tells her, get the fuck out of the car, you fuck. She says something about fuck you, you're taking me fuckin' home. When I get closer I see he's trying to push her out. I stop there, hoping a witness might put a cap on their fight, and I notice a sticker on his windshield from the Policemen's Benevolent Association. In the second it takes for him to look at me, I try to let him know I'm there for the girl's protection. The guy goes to the passenger side and tries to pull the girl out of the car. She's going, get your fuckin' hands off me, he's going, you're fuckin' walkin' home, bitch. A bouquet of flowers comes flying from the car and hits the guy on his head. I think, that's a classic, she should follow that up by throwing a drink in his face. Now he starts talking to me—asking about what the fuck I'm looking at. I say, you tell *me* what I'm looking at. Then I think, what did I just say? He walks over to me, his girl yelling about how he should pick on someone his own size. She was full of clichés, this one. He says, I'll tell you what you're lookin' at, and I think, here we fuckin' go. You're lookin' at an ass kickin'. If you don't mind your own business and get the fuck out of here, that's what you're lookin' at.

Yeah? I say. Whose ass?

The guy asks me what the fuck my problem is and shoves me in the chest with one arm. I grab his wrist with my right hand and land my left elbow on his nose. God knows where I learned it. After we each throw a few useless punches, I get his head in my armpit and hear his girl yell, get the fuck off him. I try to knee him in the crotch. I want to break his goddamn prick so he can never fuck anything again. I get one clean shot. The top of my foot lands perfectly between his legs and the guy is done. There is no more battle from him; he just stays down on the street trying to cover up. I guess I kind of lose it for a second because I don't even hear the cops pull up, I just feel a billy club against my throat.

I'D SNEAK IN to see Roseanna after work, usually. On the weekends the bar would close about two or three in the morning. I would restock the bar and leave after last call, before lockup. This was the part of the evening we used to call slim-pick hour. The only people who were left in the place were those who were still looking to hook up with someone—anyone—or those who would suck down two more to be sauced up to the point where all they could do was pour themselves out of their car if they survived the ride home.

There were two fights at work that night. This was about a month before Roseanna went out West. First fight, the bouncers separated two girls who were holding each other by their hair. One bouncer tucked one of the girls under his arm like a football and carried her out to the street, where she tumbled over and ripped her stockings in eighteen places. From the ground, this girl delivered the most vile combination of obscenities about a bouncer's mother I ever heard. The bouncer casually unhooked one end of the barrier rope, then the other. He held the two ends together in one hand and—once and hard—whipped the girl with the velvet loop, then walked back into the bar.

The next fight, about an hour and a half later, a guy took a chair to the back of the head. When the bouncers approached the malook who did it, he put one hand in the inside of his jacket and said, don't you dare. At which point, the bouncers schlepped the malook outside and explained to him their gun policy. When the guy who was hit came to, he wanted to know who hit him. The bouncer's reply: Sonny Corleone.

With a wad of singles in my sneaker and a what-the-fuck-is-up-with-this-place-I-live-in thought in my head, I drove to Roseanna's.

The candle was lit and she was sleeping. I sat on the floor with my back against her dresser, looking at her. She always slept with her eyes slightly open. Down near her bottom lid you could see white and a trace of green. But it was too dark in the room to see it then. It was two-thirty in the morning, snowing, I was a teenager and my girlfriend was naked under her covers waiting for me. For a moment the whole damn city shut its fucking mouth for once. It put its bottles and fists down and before it delivered another shot of booze or rage, presented me with a rarefied gift. A picture that would be branded into my retinas for when I finally left this place. Whenever that would be. A thoughtful going-away present. I prayed that when I was in my forties and remembered this moment, it would make me feel like a teenager again and not a hundred years old.

I noticed the handles of the dresser drawer had been digging into my back. So I stood up, unwrapped the scarf from my neck, put it next to her pillow and left. The next morning she called me and said she had something of mine and would I come over tonight and get it.

THE COPS SEPARATE us and try to get the story. They call the guy by his first name—Rick. Fuck, they know the guy. Rick's girlfriend is telling them how I landed the first punch and her boyfriend didn't do anything. I say he was hitting her. Rick doesn't deny the fight but says he never laid a hand on her. Girlfriend backs him. They tell the cops they saw me come out of the bar and now they got me for underage drinking, also. It's clear to everyone that I'm in the wrong place and don't know the right policemen.

On the way to the precinct the cops call me pretty boy and want to know if that's how I pick up all my chicks. They ask me twice if I had enough fun tonight. I know better than to answer either time. They say, the night ain't over and tomorrow is gonna be even more fun when you get your cheese sandwich for breakfast.

ROSEANNA AND I actually met on the street. I was in a bar with a group of guys and that particular night I wasn't into it. I was bored and sad, really. So I left early, after the first drink. I was walking out to the parking lot and noticed her walking in front of me. This car passed us and someone threw a bottle against the wall just for fun. We each stopped to see if the other was OK. We were strangers but took each other in quickly. I said, "All the winners are out tonight."

She said, "Same as last night."

There's some controversy over who asked whom for whose phone number first. Nevertheless, I called her the next night. She was three years older than I was, a year ago had graduated from Catholic high school and was now a biology major at Saint John's University in Queens. Her parents didn't want her to go away to school. Turns out, the night we met, she cut out early on her friends, too.

Sometimes we would drive deeper north, into the suburbs. We found this park on the Hudson River a few miles above the Tappan Zee Bridge. At night we would hop the fence, sit by the bank and drink wine from the bottle. She would name obscure cities and make me guess the countries they were in. I was never as good at that game as I wanted to be.

Her family hated me. That might be too strong. Ignored me, is fair. I was way too American. Yeah, my name was Joseph Frascone and my grandparents spoke the same language as they did, but I still wasn't Italian enough. What kind of self-respecting, Neapolitan family would let their son walk around with hair halfway down his back, four earrings and holes in his jeans? He must be American. I was never acknowledged as the boyfriend. I was always just one of Roseanna's friends whom they prayed would, eventually, stop coming around. Her family had better plans for her. They were set to marry her off to some guy from the other side. Every family function they would try and hook her up with someone new. Someone worthy. Someone un-American. I was denied the pleasure of attending such functions and watching forty-year-old men with the aroma of anisette on their breath try to walk off with my girlfriend. I always missed all the fun. But I'd get the call later those nights. You had to see the Dago clown they had for me this time, she would say. Guy was on me like a halo on a statue.

Being from Italy, Roseanna's parents were afraid of what America would do to their daughter. And, like any other parents, they could only teach their daughter what they knew. What they knew was that the woman was supposed to find a man who could make enough money to get a house, food and maybe some nice things. The food was to be prepared by the woman; the nice things and the house were to be kept by her. Roseanna had to find a guy like that. Yonkers wasn't a dead-end place if that was Roseanna's goal, but that wasn't her goal. Although Roseanna did find moments of acceptance for the traditional ways her family lived. She spent her one weekend out of the year in a housedress and a kerchief, jarring tomatoes for sauce. And liked it. But as a lifestyle it simply wasn't her choice. She wanted to travel to places like Egypt, Africa, Australia and spend some time in the western part of America. And who knows, maybe one day get a charming one-bedroom apartment in Manhattan or a cabin in the mountains. She said she maybe wanted to be a veterinarian.

My mother sensed the maternal void Roseanna grew up with and treated her with a trust and openness that only a mother could. In my house, if Roseanna wanted something to drink, she was told to get it herself. At the end of a meal, she was to wash the dishes like the rest of us. Before my mother went to bed, she would kiss Roseanna good night, as she would her own daughter.

If Roseanna needed counsel, she went right to my mother. Sometimes even circumventing me. Roseanna ate that maternal thing right up. It worked out well for my mother, also, because it had been a long time since I'd come to her with a desire to be reassured or coddled in that way. Any kind of parental void my sister and I might have grown up with, we tried to fill internally or with each other.

Even though I was only sixteen and Roseanna was nineteen, my mother allowed her to sleep at our house on the old couch we had in our basement. Of course, those nights we'd often get a call from Roseanna's friend Donna, who would say that Roseanna's mother called to check up on her and that Roseanna should get back to her when she got out of the bathroom. Easy enough.

One day my mother brought home a puppy—a tiny Dalmatian one of our neighbors was trying to find a home for. I asked my mother if she was going to keep her and she said, we'll see. Later on that night, Roseanna came over and melted at the sight of the little dog. It was mutual. The dog was the only creature in the room who could match Roseanna's energy.

Roseanna goes, "She looks like a little yin yang."

I said, "That's a great name."

My mother said, "Merry Christmas three months early."

A COP APPROACHES the cell. Thank Christ, I know the guy. His name is Stanley. He used to take the calls at the bar I worked at. So I saw him a lot. His name got me out of a speeding ticket once and I'm relieved to see him approach, thinking he's maybe gotten me out of this. I say, hey, Stanley. He tells me the guy I fought was Richard DePasquale, a sergeant detective's son. I say, shit. He says, yeah. He also asks what the fight was about. I try to explain. I ask him if he can help me out. He says he's gonna try but can't do anything until he gets the word from DePasquale. As he walks away, I'm tempted to ask him to stay with me for a while.

THE FIRST TIME the brother kicked me out, Roseanna and I were in the basement watching a movie. He came downstairs, kicked the door open like he was in an old-time western and said, Roseanna, it's late. He was a punk playing man of the house.

She said, "It's ten-thirty, Vince."

"I don't wanna hear no back talk. And you know what I'm sayin'."

I said, "If you want me to leave, Vince, you could just ask me."

He said, "I'm going upstairs."

At the door, Roseanna said to me, "My brother can be a real—"

I told her it was cool, it was no problem.

She said, "Yeah, for you."

The second time he tried to kick me out, the whole neighborhood heard it.

He came down to the basement. "Roseanna, what the hell is going on?"

I stood up and made for my coat.

"What's your problem, Vince?"

Oh, shit, I thought. *She's gonna fight him on this one.*

"What's *my* problem?"

"Yeah, you come in here like you're my father, kick my friends out—"

"It's late. Your friends can visit during the day."

"My friends can come whenever the fuck they want."

"Watch your goddamn mouth."

"Nice language, Vincent."

"Why you being such a bitch?"

"I'm a bitch? You can't open up your mouth without barking out orders for me, and then when I try to defend myself, I'm a bitch."

"You're never gonna learn."

"Fuck you, Vince!"

"No, fuck you, Roseanna."

Here we go. The mother came downstairs. In her broken English, "What are you two doing? What's going on?"

"Your daughter's being a bitch."

"Don't talk about your sister like that."

"Fuck you, Vince."

"Don't curse at your brother."

Yin Yang the puppy started barking. Roseanna's face got red and she was screaming through tears now. "Fuck this whole fucking place." Into the bedroom, she grabbed a backpack.

"What are you doing?" her mother yelled.

"I'm doing what I should've done a long time ago!"

Vince goes, "Yeah, OK, run away, that's a good one. You won't last a day out there."

"Fuck you, Vince, you fucking asshole—"

"Don't say that to your brother!"

"I'm gonna do so much better out there than your sorry ass will ever fuckin' do."

"You wish."

The father came down and screamed like a three-hundred-pound tenor. "ROSEANNA! YOU DON'T LEAVE THIS HOUSE."

Roseanna said, "All of a sudden you notice I'm here."

"YOU DON'T LEAVE THIS HOUSE." He thought his stature was going to rule, that everyone would shut up when they heard his wrath.

"I'm fucking leaving."

Roseanna pulled a sweatshirt over her head so hard that she hit her bottom lip into her teeth and drew blood.

Vince said, "Stop this bullshit."

"I am. I'm stopping this bullshit right now."

The tenor ineffectively screamed "Roseanna" again. The mother came over to me, trying to be polite and calm, and said, "Joseph, please just go."

Roseanna said, "No! He does what he wants!"

That was it. Running away was one thing, siding with me was

another. It really pissed Vince off. "Don't you ever talk to your mother that way."

The fight moved to the front door. I went out first and stayed on the stoop while Roseanna stood in the open doorway telling her family what kind of bastards she thought they were. Her brother said, "Don't you dare leave this house," and grabbed her by her arm. For the first time in a long time, I wanted to kick someone in his throat. Between Roseanna pushing him and the mother pulling him, Vince let go.

"You touch me again, Vincent, I'll have you killed." She was calm now. Scary calm. She looked him down. "Don't you fuckin' follow me out here. Leave me the fuck alone."

We both got into my car and Yin Yang ran between the mother's legs and jumped through the passenger's side. Roseanna's sentence was up early, although not gracefully.

My mother was sleeping when we got to my house. I went into her room and said, "Mom, Roseanna is here."

She said, "OK," wondering why I had to wake her up to tell her that.

Then I said, "And Yin Yang is here, too."

"Yin Yang?"

"Yeah, we'll be in the basement, so don't worry. I'll explain tomorrow."

She let out a sigh, too tired to do anything else.

When I got downstairs, Roseanna was on the couch, still crying. I said, "You can stay here for a while." I brought her a box of tissues. The dog was being quiet. She put her hands on my face and I could taste the blood on her lips. When she eventually fell asleep, I was sitting up. Her head was in my lap and her eyes were slightly open.

Three weeks later she would be waiting tables in Phoenix, Arizona. But stayed at our place for the whole three weeks before she left. It was so natural, her being there. I didn't want her to go. But what kind of guy would I be if I asked her to stay in a town like this with a family like that, which she clearly needed to get away from? I wasn't going to be the guy who asked her to do that, and apparently I wasn't the guy she was going to stay for, either.

IT'S CLOSE TO three in the morning now and I'm not calling anyone. I hope Stanley can help me out. I think about Roseanna all the way in Arizona. I think about the conversation on the phone we had earlier tonight. She told me how beautiful the mountains and the Grand Canyon are. And the dog liked it out there, also. She enrolled in a community college, planning to get two semesters of kick-ass grades, then transfer to ASU. It was vet school after that. She said she misses me but she doesn't miss Yonkers. Then she apologized for waiting until then to tell me something.

He would come into my room and I would fight him off, she said. I gave him a black eye once and almost kicked him unconscious another time. One night my parents woke up and thought it was only a brother and sister fighting—that's all they thought it was. That's why I moved into the basement. Then it just stopped. I should have told you before, Joey. I'm sorry.

I feel like such a fucking moron. I'm not even a fighter. Last time was when I was riding with my buddy Mark and he got tough with this guy pulling into the diner parking lot. Mark was like, you cut me off, now you wanna go ahead of me? The guy called Mark an asshole and we all jumped out of our cars. Mark landed him one punch. I got the guy in a full nelson, his feet barely on the ground, jerking him out of the way of more punches. I was yelling to the guy to get back in his car before he got hurt. The guy's girlfriend stood with one foot still in their car, with a cigarette held involuntarily at her waist. I never threw a punch. Someone cuts me off while I'm driving, I'm not gonna hit the friggin' idiot. Hasn't the city of Yonkers endured enough machismo for one century? These fucking guys will fight about anything. I hadn't hit someone since kindergarten, for stealing a quarter from my sister.

Tonight was a different story. The phone call from Arizona put me in an unfamiliar place. Revenge. Which, in turn, put me here. And I know exactly what this looks like. I look like some schmuck who had nothing better to do tonight then to get fist-happy off a couple drinks and pounce on the first guy I saw, who happened to be the son of a sergeant detective. Maybe I hit the wrong guy. Maybe I shouldn't have hit anyone. I needed to do something. I just couldn't let it go.

I look at my hands and my mind goes to a place I never thought it would. I wonder if, in the disorientation of a late night, she ever mistook these hands for someone else's? I had a feeling I was capable of many things, but I never thought I'd be asking a question like, *Did she ever think I was him?* Now I feel like the rest of these fuckin' animals. Maybe I'm exactly where I belong. What else don't I know about family? What else don't I know about love? About myself? I don't know. I just sit here.

I want to turn around and see Roseanna looking back at me from outside the cell. I want her to go to the gate and find it's unlocked. I want her to step inside and close it slowly so no one hears her. I want her to take my hand, lead me off this bench and to the floor. I want her to put her mouth against my ear and tell me that she's all right, that it's over. I want to tell her that I miss her and make her believe that she could have told me. And when she puts her hand on the back of my head, tells me about how she's going to get me out of this place, how easy it is and how I shouldn't be afraid, I want to be able to say, I believe you. I definitely believe you.

Bleachers: An often unroofed outdoor grandstand for seating spectators. [From comparing a person's exposure to the sun when sitting in them with the exposure of linens bleaching on a clothesline.] From Old English root *bhel-,* **to shine brightly, to thrive, to bloom.**

—*American Heritage Dictionary, 1992*

This was after being unable to speak a civil word to each other since the split. After sitting on opposite sides of the gymnasium during each one of their children's school plays, or opposite sides of the field at every softball and baseball game. This was after all the stories my sister and I had heard about whose fault it was. Stories about who cheated on whom, who was the bigger fuckup with money, who lied, who hit whom, who burned whom with an iron, which one called the cops on the other one, and how one was simply annoyed by the way the other swallowed vitamins. This was after the time when I was six and I was on the phone with one parent. I was standing on a stepstool, playing with the hook latch that hung off the screen door. The stepstool slipped out from under me, and as I fell, the hook latch cut me bad between my thumb and forefinger. I bled, I screamed and a voice yelled out from the receiver as it dangled on its cord. The other parent ran in, picked me up, saw that I needed stitches, grabbed the phone and, without explaining to the voice on the other end what had happened, hung it up.

This was after all the times my sister and I were told which one of our parents we were exactly like.

THE FIRST TIME was at my sister Catherine's graduation. Twenty-two years after our parents had broken up. Catherine was the first out of the twelve cousins in our generation to receive a master's degree, so it was a big deal. Everyone in the whole family wanted to go. Problem was, my sister was only given three tickets to the ceremony. Not four or six or two, but three. No exceptions. And Catherine and I thought it was funny. She said, "Do you fuckin' believe this? That they have to go *together*? You think they'll sit with each other?"

"Yeah," I said. "Because if they don't, then they leave me to decide which one I want to sit with. I mean, they're fucked up, but they're not *that* fucked up."

We walked into the college gymnasium together. Not counting infancy, that was the first time I was ever alone with my mother and my father. Seating for families was on the bleachers, and to get to the empty seats we had to climb up six rows. I led. The bleacher steps were tall. After taking two steps, I looked back and saw that my mother (all five feet and one inch of her) was having trouble climbing. My father offered her his hand.

She took it.

I sat between them and, after many moments of silence, asked them if they were proud of their daughter.

THE SECOND TIME was at the rehearsal dinner for my sister's wedding. After each parent requested to be the only one to walk the bride down the aisle, Catherine told them that they were both going to do it. She told me before she told them. "I've had enough," she said. "I'm sick of having to choose." During the rehearsal they practiced the walk down the aisle. My sister had our father on her right arm and our mother on her left arm. This was the only time I had ever remembered seeing those three together. The rehearsal went well. My mother and my father didn't say a word to each other, but it went well.

It also ended earlier than was expected, so we had an hour to kill before our dinner reservations. The groomsmen and the bridesmaids were just standing around their cars in the church parking lot. Then someone pulled out a Wiffle ball and bat from his trunk, and to pass the time, a six-on-six game started up. My mother didn't want to play, so she sat on someone's front fender and watched.

Catherine and I were on the same team and our father pitched for the other team. He was ecstatic to be on the mound for his daughter's rehearsal dinner game and was calling play-by-play with his thicker-than-usual Bronx accent. His accent gets thicker under two circumstances: when he's happy, or when he's in a rage. He was so happy that day that everything out of his mouth was, "deez," "dem" and "dat." Saying, "Whuda youz doin'? Could we get a batta' at duh plate, or what?" When one of the groomsmen came to the plate and stuck the bat out between his legs, my father yelled, "Tommy, not in fronna' duh church, please! He's all class, dis guy!" Dad's curveball was breaking pretty well that day, but I reached second twice and took one of his curves deep to left-center over my cousin's Chrysler for a home run.

In the third inning Tommy was up again and I was on deck. Among all the screaming, laughing and busted-up accents coming from the game, nobody noticed that my mother had gotten up and walked to the edge of the parking lot. She stood staring out at the traffic, her arms folded over her chest, her back to the game. I sneaked over to her and said, "Ma, what are you doin'?"

"I'm just looking at the church."

I pointed behind her. "That one?"

She turned around and said, "Yeah."

"Listen, you gotta bat."

"Why?"

" 'Cause we need a pinch hitter."

She looked over at my father on the mound while he razzed the crowd with his charisma and his shiny shoes.

Mom said, "I don't know, Joey."

"Oh, shit." I said. "See, Tommy just struck out. We need you."

"Well . . . what do I have to do?"

"You gotta pinch-hit," I said. "Come on."

I brought her to the field.

"OK, listen up!" I yelled. "We're bringing in our pinch hitter!"

My father yelled back at me, "Whudda you? Scared a duh heat comin' off duh mound?"

I said, "No, I'm on the disabled list."

I winked at Catherine and she smiled at me as if to say, *This is gonna be good*.

Our mother got up to the plate and drew a laugh from the crowd when, in her lovely red dress, she pretended to fix her crotch and spit out a wad of chewing tobacco. She settled in the batter's box and shook her butt. The way I imagine she did when she was a young girl in the Bronx, growing up fast, walking with her friends from her parents' house down to the schoolyard to get in the game and try to impress the boy she had a crush on. With one shake of her ass in the batter's box of a church parking lot, my mother dropped thirty years.

The first pitch was on the high outside corner—my mom took an off-balanced swing at it and missed.

Someone from the outfield yelled, "No batter, no batter!"

Somebody else said, "Wait for your pitch! Don't let 'em rouse ya."

The second pitch was another swing and a miss.

Someone said, "She's swattin' flies up there! You could catch a cold from dat breeze!"

"Shut up," one of our teammates yelled back. "It was a lousy pitch! This guy can't hit the side of a van."

"You mean the side of a barn!" somebody yelled.

"OK, a barn, I don't give a shit; whatever it is, your pitcher can't hit it."

"Is that how you talk in God's house?"

"You mean in God's *parking lot*?"

The third pitch was right over the plate. Mom swung again and . . . crack! A nice little hit! A ground ball right back to the pitcher's mound! But my mother didn't run. She was shocked that she had even connected with the off-speed pitch. She stayed in the batter's box and watched my father pick up the ball; but then he just stood there, apparently too surprised that she had hit off him. Her teammates were screaming, "Run! Go! Run to first!" And the first baseman was yelling, "Come on, throw to first! Easy out, easy out!"

Mom didn't run and Dad didn't throw. They both just stood there for a moment looking very surprised, looking very young, looking as though they forgot, for one moment, what the rules of the game had always been.

AFTER WE LEFT YONKERS
AND BEFORE WE CAME BACK

n high school we used to hang out on The Bridge. It was a highway overpass. To our left, the Yonkers Raceway; under us, Interstate 87, also called the Major Deegan Expressway, which led to New York City. You'll have to ask someone else who Major Deegan was. We never asked.

From The Bridge we had a view of the Manhattan skyline. Presiding over this skyline made us feel like we were actually doing something with our time, other than killing half a night and a full case of beer. It made us feel like we were almost in New York City, therefore almost productive, almost important, almost worldly and almost even wise. The eighteen-wheelers that would drive under us were tall enough to create an illusion that they were actually going to hit The Bridge. We would lean over the traffic just to feel the rush of possible danger. Even after doing this countless times, the illusion never wore off. And, not to disparage the girls we grew up with in Yonkers, but we thought taking them to the bridge, showing them the New York City skyline and the trucks that were about to smash into us, would impress the shit out of them. And it almost did.

Almost.

We were so close to the greatest city in the world. And almost being in the city was all we had. That's what it felt like to me, at least. I was so close to being somewhere great. I couldn't figure out how to be in love with the place I was growing up in, but I knew I had to be in love with something. I needed to find some practical philosophy that would allow me to live the way I knew I could. I wasn't happy to be in high school. I wasn't happy to be in Yonkers. I wasn't willing to stay around and see what new and exciting thing would roll off I-87 beckoning me to join it. I mean, come on. The only things that ever rolled off I-87 were trucks that were never quite tall enough to smash the illusion on which I was standing.

There was one simple truth in all this, waiting to be discovered: When you're miserable you have two choices. You can change the scenery or change your relationship to the scenery. Of course, changing your relationship to the scenery entails looking into yourself. What did we know about looking into ourselves? So I came up with something much simpler. Get the hell out of Yonkers. Of course, I couldn't figure out how to do even this by myself. I needed company.

Mark and Benny became my company. And this is really their story, which started years before I met them.

MARK ZADOTTI AND Benny Colangelo grew up on the same block in the Odell section of Yonkers. Odell was right between north Yonkers and south Yonkers. Not uptown or downtown, not rich or poor, just a working-class neighborhood existing between other neighborhoods. They went to the same elementary school and junior high. I lived on the north side of Yonkers and didn't meet either of them until high school. By the time I got to Mark and Benny, they were already packing fourteen years of history. As I spent more time with them, I saw that history come out. There was this thing that Benny used to do to Mark—midsentence, apropos of nothing (other than that he could), Benny would grab Mark by his earlobe and in a shrill falsetto voice say, "*Lemme get a little bit.*" It always annoyed Mark; it always made him laugh. It made both of them laugh. It made all of us laugh.

They would also fight. I don't mean they were giving each other black eyes or even threatening to. They never put their hands on each other in anger. But they did fight like brothers. Meaning, sometimes they would fight for no other reason besides their proximity to each other. Or that they each always wanted their own fucking way. They would fight for status, they would fight over nothing, they would fight just because they wanted to fight somebody. And, like brothers, they would eventually stop fighting, sit down and eat together again.

Mark drove a 1982 green Buick Regal, a two-door sedan. Its exterior and interior were so offensively green that it came dangerously close to looking like a mobile pimp unit. It didn't help that the windows were tinted past the legal limit and that Mark kept a cylinder of bathroom air freshener on the dashboard. We loved this car like a family member and better than some. Today, when we speak of that time, it is known as the Green Regal Era. We identify many eras in our lives that way. There was the Blue Suede Puma Era, the Lee Pinstripe Jean Era, and the Paco Raban Era.

Mark lived in a house with his mother, his stepfather and his half-sister (who was a Green Regal Era baby.) I met Mark in Mr. Goldberg's tenth-grade level one Italian class, and sensed immediately that he, like me, was looking to make a move. It wasn't that he was having a miserable time with life. He was not a depressive character. He was charming, funny and had a smile like a fake ID that always got him in. The day his half-sister was born, he came to school with a box of cigars. When he would say goodbye to people, leaving a room, a pizza place, or a classroom, his staple farewell was, *"Enjoy."* And he'd give a military salute when he said it, as if it were our sworn duty to enjoy, as if we could get through this war, even as privates, if we could just have some goddamn fun around here.

Mark was lighter than I was about where he was and what he was doing, but he also wanted to get out of it. He made where we were (Yonkers, New York, ages fifteen through seventeen) better by confirming the idea that breaking out of our place and ourselves was an honorable endeavor.

When did I first meet Benny? I couldn't tell you exactly. Just one random day in school when Mark introduced us, or maybe one afternoon when we rode over to Benny's house in the Green Regal. I didn't know much about his family. He wasn't very open about it. I knew that his father had left his mother when Benny was about seven years old—went to Connecticut to open a restaurant and live in a big house with another woman. Other than that, Benny didn't talk much about his dad or the fact that his parents had split. It's not as if he didn't have people around to talk about it with. Mark and I also came from broken homes. My parents hadn't lived together or even talked to each other for nearly my whole life. It was the same story with Mark. We bitched and raged about it all the time together. We broke beer bottles and punched walls over it. We played songs and took long rides because of it. Together, we created a great place to let that shit loose. Benny never joined us in this. If he had, maybe the three of us could have been the perfect trifecta of healing. But Benny never went there with us. I don't know if he didn't *want* to talk about, or felt he *couldn't,* or thought he wasn't *supposed* to. Bottom line is, he didn't.

And here's what little I knew about Benny's mother.

I never actually met her face-to-face. I was never sure why. There were things I felt I didn't have the right to ask about Benny. I hadn't put in the kind of time that Mark had with him and I just thought I would learn all I needed to learn as time went on. But Benny's mother I never found out about.

I do remember pulling up to Benny's house with Mark one night, ringing his doorbell.

Mark said, "He's not here."

"Is that his light on?"

"No. That's his mother's."

"She trying to fool the thieves?"

"No, she's home. She's always home."

"How come she doesn't answer the door?"

"She never does. She's a little out of it."

"How's that, now?"

"Just . . . I don't know. Just out of it."

Another time a bunch of us were playing cards in Benny's kitchen. We had the air conditioner on and it blew a fuse. The lights in the whole house went off. That was the first time I actually heard Benny's mother's voice. She started to scream for him.

Benito! Vene ca! Vene ca, Benito!

Benny jumped up from the table. We heard him feeling through a junk drawer. "Mark," he said, "go down to the basement and flip the circuit breaker. Hurry." With a flashlight Benny ran first to the air conditioner to turn it off, then upstairs. The rest of us looked at each other in the spill of the streetlight as we heard Benny reassuring his mother in Italian. She was crying. There was a soft tone in his voice. A sound I had never heard him use before. Mark found the breaker and got the lights on. We could tell Benny's mother had started to calm down because he was now speaking to her in English. Mark came up from the basement as Benny came downstairs. I asked if everything was OK and if his mother needed any help. Benny announced adamantly that the game would now continue with the windows open.

He sat back down at the table, looked at me and said, "Deal, bitch."

SO WHAT DID we do? With all our talk and desire about how great we wanted to be, what did we do all day long? School? School we went to . . . often. Often enough to pass. But it was so easy not to go. The Yonkers public school system wasn't too tight. If we cut a day, our parents didn't get a phone call. If we cut thirty or forty days, then they would probably get a call. Mark used to drive us to school, to Roosevelt High School on the corner of Tuckahoe Road and Central Park Avenue. Central Park Avenue branched off Interstate

87. Our school was about seven miles north of The Bridge. We would approach Roosevelt from Tuckahoe Road. There was a hill at the last stretch of the drive. When we got to the top of the hill we had our first view of the school. This was called Decision Hill.

I cut school just as much as they did, but I had a sick feeling about it that I kept to myself. Maybe I felt bad because I was dishonoring my parents' wishes for me to be educated and responsible. Or because my older sister always did so well in school and always seemed to enjoy it, not only on an academic level but a social one. I did not. Maybe I felt bad because there were some smart and good teachers there who were willing to pass knowledge on to me and I didn't take them up on it. Or maybe it was because I knew I was a really good baseball player and never tried out. Maybe a combination of all those things churned my secret sickness. But there was still that one thing that kept gnawing at me. It was an idea that turned into a credo; it consumed me. The idea was that I wasn't supposed to make it work where I was. What was right for me was somewhere else.

MARK ZADOTTI AND Benny Colangelo appeared to have their own ideas and demons that led them to believe they should've been somewhere else doing something else, too. Our similar convictions manifested in a lot of beer-drinking, a lot of time spent on The Bridge, a lot of Green Regal cruising and a lot of time cutting class. Yes, we had jobs. Benny and I both worked in restaurants as waiters and Mark worked in a sporting goods store. Still, all day long, in the city of Yonkers, from age fifteen through seventeen, we weren't doing all that much.

Mind you, there were also girls.

First of all, here's what each of us looked like. Mark and I fit the same physical description: tall, dark hair, dark eyes, muscular. We were good-looking and knew this but somehow knew better than to abuse it. We were easy on the eyes, and that carried a lot of weight in our neighborhood, but we had sense enough to know that if we were to be put in a room full of *truly* beautiful people, we would be asked to leave.

Benny's description was different. Short, light hair that went from blond to red depending on how the traffic lights hit it, and hazel eyes. He also had, even at that young age, a tiny bald spot brewing, and he talked a lot about wanting to lose weight.

Benny loved us even though he had a little trouble coping with our looks. He had a history of getting pissed off at guys he thought were better-looking than him. He was no moron; he already noticed that good looks were a passport in this world, a free ticket. He knew he needed a different kind of passport. Therefore he would never back down to anyone. If you opened Benny's passport, it would have read, "The more balls you got, the more you get away with."

One night, we were driving around some neighborhood in south Yonkers trying to find a bar Benny had heard about that was supposed to be "populated" with hot chicks. But he'd only heard *about* this place. He hadn't heard where it was located. As the search entered its second hour, Mark was about to kill Benny. "If you don't get us to this fucking bar in two fucking minutes, there's gonna be a Green Regal *beating*." At the next red light, a car full of tough guys pulled alongside us. In his frustration Mark said, "Why don't you ask these dicks where this shit is?" Benny rolled down the window of the Green Regal, got the other driver's attention and yelled "Hey, dick? Where's the shit?"

At the restaurant where Benny worked, he would argue with the chef a lot. He hated this guy. One night they got into it bad and Benny decided he'd had enough. In front of the whole kitchen staff and a general manager, at five-foot-six and sixteen years of age, Benny Colangelo was able to control his rage enough to pick up a kitchen knife and hand it to the chef, handle facing toward him, the safe way. The chef said, "What's that for?"

"Take it." Benny said. The chef did. "If you're gonna talk to me like that," Benny continued, "you're gonna need this. Now it's a fair fight."

Then Benny punched the guy once in his face. The chef dropped the knife. Benny hit him again and the chef ran out of the kitchen. Benny could have forgone the whole knife thing and kicked his ass much worse than he did. It's just that he liked to be creative with his violence.

Mark went through girls on a fairly regular basis. There always seemed to be someone on the way in or on the way out. I myself had a steady girlfriend at the time. Holly. An adorable five-foot-nothing Irish girl with blond hair and the world's most killer smile. She was from Scarsdale, a rich suburb. We met while both working at the same restaurant. We were walking out of the place one night and she said to me, "By the way, could I kiss you?" I was with Holly for the better part of the Green Regal Era. Mark and Benny liked Holly because you couldn't not, and we always liked the girls Mark would hook up with. When we had time to get to know them, that is.

So, as far as girls were concerned, it went like this: Mark always got the girl, I always had the girl and Benny hated both of us for it. However, that equation could get evened out for twenty bucks and a ride to 30th and 11th Avenue in Manhattan.

Benny and Mark had a ball with these hookers, but the only reasons I went were to take a ride to Manhattan with my friends, get out of Yonkers for the night and be the lookout man on the street. I never participated in anything more than that and Mark and Benny respected it. Holly, and all that. Those nights worked out so well. There was no jealousy, no anger and no teenage-bullshit-game-playing to try and get down someone's pants. The best part was that we all looked the same to those girls, or at least they treated us as if we did.

One night, though, I took the trip myself.

I drove to the city and when I got to 30th Street between 10th and 11th I pulled up to a woman who said, "You want a blow job, baby?" She came over to the car and I held a twenty-dollar bill in my fingers.

"Would you just hang out and talk to me for a few minutes?"

"Sure, baby."

She got into the car and let out a sigh that thanked me for giving her a break and a warm place to be for a while.

"Are we OK over here?"

"Yeah, just pull outta the middle of the street. Nobody gonna bother us."

"What's your name?"

"Tanya. What's yours?"

"Joe." My own name sounded like a lie. "I just want to talk, that's OK, right?"

"Yeah, that's OK."

It now occurred to me that I had no fucking idea what to ask her.

"Man, it's freezing. Don't you get cold out here?"

"Yeah, sometimes, but I got wool tights on, so I'm OK."

"You see a lot of violence?"

"Yeah, I seen some stuff, but mostly people don't fuck with us."

"What have you seen?"

"Just some guys gettin' all tough, but they don't fuck with us."

"I guess guys get tough everywhere."

"Um-hum." This, she was sure about.

"Do guys do this, do they come down just to talk to you?"

"I talk to guys sometimes if it's not their rap. Some guys wanna come down and make themselves feel good, like they trying to save me and shit."

"You got a boyfriend?"

"I got boyfriends! Whatchu think?"

"I wasn't sure."

She laughed. The most shocking thing about Tanya was how ordinary she seemed. Like many people I knew, she chose a profession that had its good days and bad days. She kept late hours, had to dress up for work and went on dates. It was all a little dangerous, but hey, she was working with what she had. She felt familiar to me. She was a neighborhood girl. She was just walking through her scenery, somehow contented with it, not seeing how she could've ever changed it. I was fantasizing that she could give me some kind of universal wisdom and insight. I was hoping she might show me a different perspective, but she only offered a big-city version of the one I already knew.

"What was the happiest moment of your life?" I asked her. "What's the most excited you've ever been?"

"When I saw Santa Claus." Tanya answered the question indignantly, as if I were crazy for thinking that there could be any other moment in anyone's life that could top that.

"You saw Santa Claus?"

"Yeah, I saw Santa Claus. When I was little. I used to sleep in the living room where we had our tree and I saw him come in and I made like I was asleep, so he went real quiet to the tree with some presents and then he tiptoed out. And that was the happiest thing, when I saw Santa Claus. It was really my father, but I saw Santa Claus."

THERE WERE OTHER guys we hung around with. Danny Ryan, John Nolan, Frank Gianguzzi . . . But there was a certain thing that happened when only Mark, Benny and myself got together. A conversation about "what the fuck are we going to do after high school" would come up.

I like to think that kids at that age emanate their future. When you look at teenagers you could see it somewhere on them, in something they do, some skill that they are already confident about, or some way of behaving that makes them seem to already belong in a society outside of school. Clearly the other guys had their things. Gianguzzi would be a cop. Nolan could teach. Danny would own his own bar. This was all very obvious. What wasn't so obvious was what was going to become of Mark, Benny and myself.

This "what the fuck are were we going to do" conversation started to come up more often as senior year began. And it always seemed to take place over a beer, a bridge, a raceway and a skyline.

And one autumn night on The Bridge, we came up with a plan.

As usual we started off the conversation throwing out scenarios. Learn trades? Benny had a good business mind and could probably do something with that. But what exactly? Mark and I . . . we weren't college-bound. Mark saw himself going off to the Marines. This scared the shit out of me as much as it did him. Therefore, when he took the military aptitude test that they gave through the school, I took it with him. I figured it would be a goof and a free day out of class. The kick in the ass is that I wound up getting the third highest score in the city; and that's what the recruiting officers would remind me every time they called my house. *Every time.* They got to calling so much that the phone would ring during dinner and my mother would say, "Doesn't the military know we're eating?"

"Mr. Frascone, we were just wondering what your plans were after you graduate from high school."

"Well, I'm not really—"

"Did you know, on our aptitude test, that you received the third highest score in the city?"

"Dude, the third highest score in the city of *Yonkers*. Don't get so excited. I don't think I'm what you're looking for. I got ripped jeans, long hair and four earrings. You guys really should relax."

Mark got the same kind of calls.

Actually doing something like joining the military was appealing only because it was so friggin' outlandish. But that still would've been choice by default. That wouldn't have been making the kind of choice we wanted; it would have been choosing from what was available. That was unacceptable and terrifying. So what the fuck? Where *was* the really good stuff? Where was all the stuff that matched up to what was going on inside us?

These questions led us—in our senior year of high school, at the height of the Green Regal Era—to the plan. Leave in January and drive across America.

The "leave in January" part was the beauty of it.

How we were going to do this was almost more important than what we were actually going to do. Leaving in January meant dropping out of high school. We couldn't just wait five months until graduation and then take the summer to go bouncing around the country. No. It had to be a little more dramatic than that. We knew what people would say. That we would be throwing away our fine potential, writing ourselves off as dregs of society, walking around for the rest of our lives without high school diplomas. Our thinking was so contrary. We were looking for a rebel's and a hero's send-off. We were trying to plant evidence in the school, in the town, in our families and with our friends that proved we were different, evidence that pointed to the fact that we would never be the same after this—indeed that we had never been the same as them in the first place. Yeah, we could've finished off the last half of the school year and been done with it, but we were seventeen and we needed something to remember ourselves by.

It was a beautiful plan.

LEAVING SCHOOL UNNOTICED was obviously not a problem—we'd been doing it for years already and the Yonkers public school system hadn't demonstrated too much concern about it yet. Not to mention that we were all seventeen, which made it legal. Of course, there were our parents. Mark's parents let him go only if he would agree with them that he was crazy. So, he did. My father was cool with it. He said it was something he wished he had done when he was my age. Or any age. My mother put up a fight. But after a few weeks of explanation and negotiation, I promised her that, at some point, I would get a high school diploma. Benny's father didn't have much to say about it. Or anything to say about it. I don't know what Benny needed to tell his mother in order to leave, although Mark might have known. I did ask Benny.

"You tell your mom you were going?"

"Yeah."

"What'd she say?"

"Nothing."

I really wanted him to tell me what that nothing was.

"She gonna be all right?" I said.

"She's already all right."

I stopped right there.

WE NEEDED A van. We wanted something big enough to sleep in. We were going to split the cost three ways. We would each throw in about a grand. Benny and I could make it on our tips and Mark on what he brought in at the store. Also, he would have to sell the Green Regal.

After looking for a few weeks, we found a van that seemed to be it. We had to take a ride to Long Island to check it out. That day, Benny and I were outside Mark's house, throwing a football over the Regal, waiting for Mark to get his shit together.

Benny said, "What the fuck do you do?"

"What do you mean?"

"How the fuck do you look like that *all the time*?"

Innocently I said, "Like *what*?"

Sarcastically he said, "Like what."

"I do push-ups. I run."

"That's all you fucking do? *Push-ups?* How many *push-ups* do you do?"

"Like, a hundred."

"That's all you fuckin' do is a hundred fuckin' push-ups and you fuckin' look like *that*? *In a row?*"

"No. In a day." This seemed to me like a good place for the conversation to end. Benny didn't see it that way.

"In a *day*? Like, you drop ten times a day and do ten push-ups?"

"No. I do like fifty and fifty."

"*Bullshit.* You can't do fifty at once."

"I can."

"You can't do fifty push-ups."

I gave him a look as if to say, *Don't believe me,* and he stopped throwing the football.

"Let me see."

"Come on, B."

"No, come on."

"Throw the ball, B."

"Lemme see."

"B."

"GO!"

When I got to about forty, his jealousy kicked in hard and he said, "I guess you can do fifty push-ups."

"So can you."

"Yeah, right."

"You can."

"Shut up."

"How many can you do?"

"Fuckin' guy . . . I could probably do, like . . . ten."

"Today. And in two months, if you worked up to it, you could do fifty. You want a trainer? I'll train your ass. By the time we leave for the trip you'll be doing fifty."

Mark came out of the house hearing the last thing I'd said. He looked at me.

"Hey, Jack LaLanne? You and your little gym buddy ready to go see a man about a van?"

We got out to Valley Stream, Long Island, where a man in his fifties was selling a 1980 Ford van. An Econoline 350, four-speed stick. It was carpeted, had two captain's chairs in the back and (this we considered a fine feature) an air horn with a pull line. We knew right off the bat that we had scored with this guy. One thing I believe we each had, even at that age, was a sense for sincerity. Personally we weren't always sincere, and that may have aided our instincts about it, but this guy was being sincere. That makes it easier when you're seventeen and about to hand someone three thousand dollars in cash. He took us for a test drive.

"In the first two gears she'll buck, but that's only till she gets warm, then she smoothes out. I never get pulled over. You know why? I ride in the middle lane, five miles over the speed limit all the time. We used to go upstate a lot, I had this house in the Adirondacks when my kids were young, and I never got pulled over. I would save *this* for anyone with silver hair doing less than forty miles an hour on Route 17."

Then he grabbed the pull line and let it rip. The damn thing was as loud as a fire truck. The guy laughed his head off. "You had to see those old schmucks jump. Excuse my language."

He looked back at us and got serious for a moment. "You'll take care of her?"

It felt right and we all knew it. Guy called his van a *she*. I mean, come on.

"Yeah, we'll take care of her."

The Green Regal Era had ended.

There were a couple things that had to be done to the van before the trip. We *had* to get a good stereo system. We got a pair of nice speakers mounted in the back and Benny had a stereo with a benzi box. Benzi-boxes allowed you to pop the stereo out from the dash quickly so you could take it with you or hide it when you were away from your car. Then there was stuff that needed to happen that we didn't even know needed to happen because we didn't know anything about cars. Like packing the bearings on the wheels? Mark's stepfather Nick was happy to let us know how ignorant we were about this. And offered to fix up the van for us at the garage he owned, for cheap. Turned out our instincts were right. Even Nick had to admit. "You guys did all right. It's like it's practically new."

Nick was a Bronx guy who moved to Yonkers when he married Mark's mother. Mark didn't have much of a relationship with his stepfather. I thought he was a typical neighborhood malook. But Benny and Nick got along famously. I think it was Nick's over-the-top manliness that attracted Benny. Nick would tell stories about literally slapping girls in the face with his dick to see whether or not they could "play with the big boys." In front of Mark's mother he would say this. He would also tell about how he and his friends used to drive around Midtown Manhattan during lunch and ask guys in suits for directions, then throw eggs at them. He attracted a particular kind of audience. Benny loved his act, but Mark had long grown tired of it. Of course, Nick had a short temper, as well. I once saw him throw a buttered piece of Italian bread against the dining room wall during a Sunday dinner because he had spilled his glass of red wine. He was saying something about the table being so crowded.

Without apology, he said, "I'm not used to eating like this."

Mark said, "What, with utensils?"

Mark's mother had cleaned up the bread and the wine while Nick changed his sweat suit.

"Watch your asses down south," he told us now, after checking out the van.

Benny said, "Nick, we're gonna fuck every beautiful girl in this country."

"Think of me when you're in the sack."

Benny laughed. Mark, who had his reasons for not laughing, said, "Thanks for checking out the van, Nick."

"Yeah. It's practically new."

IN THE FEW months before we left, Benny kept talking about getting his body looking as good as it possibly could. I kept trying to make him do push-ups, but he just wanted to talk about it. He said to me one day, "Fuck this, I'm getting huge." So he got himself on this program called Cybergenics. It was a get-big-quick plan that consisted of protein supplements, an insane amount of weight lifting and a well-monitored diet of eating the shit out of everything in your parents' house. The only restriction was that you weren't allowed to eat after eight P.M. For the first week, Benny was so serious about the program that, one night, when the three of us wound up at a diner at two o'clock in the morning, he ordered nothing while Mark and I had cheeseburger deluxes. In rare silence, Benny watched us eat. But when our waitress came by and asked if we needed anything else, Benny said, "Yeah, a cheeseburger deluxe, gravy on the fries."

That was the last we heard of Cybergenics.

"You know what we need?" Benny shouted from the shotgun position of the Green Regal, later that same night.

Mark said, "To take the ride?" That was code for go-to-Manhattan-and-pick-up-hookers.

"No," Benny said. "I mean, yeah, but no. What we need is one more Bridge night before we go."

"You think?"

"I know. I need a whole night. I need to shoot a few rounds at Roland's Pool Hall, then I need my Bridge and my boys and my raceway and some adult beverage."

Mark said, "Why?"

Benny grabbed Mark by his earlobe. "Because I need a little bit. Lemme get a little bit."

Mark, laughing: "I thought that's why we were leaving. To get away from that shit."

"Come on, one more time, just to say goodbye."

I said from the back seat, "I'd be happy to say goodbye. You kiddin' me?"

Benny reached back for my hand. "There's my boy. Where's my other boy?" Reaching for Mark's ear again: "Where's my other boy? Where is he? Where is he?"

Mark kept slapping his hand away and then finally grabbed it.

"*There's* my brother."

We headed downtown and played a final round at Roland's, then we went to say goodbye to The Bridge. Benny was bent on getting a bottle of champagne for this, but none of us had any ID that was going to hold up in a liquor store. The guys in the pool halls and the delis never gave a shit about ID when they sold us beer, but the liquor stores were different. We pulled up to the first one and Mark and I went in because we were taller and maybe looked older, but that didn't impress the guy who was working there.

"Can I see some ID?"

"I'm twenty-two."

"I still need to see some ID."

"I don't have any on me now."

"Then I can't sell to you."

"I lost my wallet. . . ."

"You lost your wallet?"

"Yeah."

"With your driver's license in it?"

"Yeah."

"Then you drove over here without a license?"

"You gotta do what you gotta do."

"That's right, kid. We all do. You understand? I'll see you guys in a couple years."

On the way out, under our breath, "No, you won't."

It's so easy to think someone is an asshole when he's getting in the way of what you want. Even if the guy is trying to protect his business, which is the financial source that supports his whole family, by not selling you the thing that you were stupid enough to bank your good time on. In that one moment of rejection, when he becomes the only thing between you and your good time, he's a real asshole.

When we got back into the car empty-handed, Benny laughed. "You fuckin' guys. Let's go to another one. I'm going in."

At the next liquor store, Mark and I watched Benny walk in. Four minutes later he walked out with a huge smile and a cheap bottle of champagne.

"Fuck did you do that?"

"How do you think?"

" 'Cause you got the key to the city?"

" 'Cause I *am* the key to the city. I got the J-U-ice, all over town. I own this bitch."

We got up to The Bridge and Benny held the neck of the bottle and pushed the cork off with his thumbs. It flew over the fence that surrounded the raceway. He yelled, "I love this town!" Then he got ready to suck the foam off the top of the bottle, but the foam never materialized.

"This *is* cheap stuff." Then Benny toasted. "To our trip and to us. You guys are it. You really are."

IT WAS JANUARY 22, 1989, and we planned to leave on January twenty-third. My eighteenth birthday. Our last night at home went like this: I had to say goodbye to Holly; Mark had to call the girl he was involved with and apologize for not being able to see her that night; Benny was going to finish out his last shift at the restaurant.

Benny said, "Ask me how much money I made tonight."

"How much, B?"

"Guess."

"Ninety."

"Again."

"More? A century?"

"More."

"Fuck outta here."

"Guess."

"Tell me."

"A buck eighty."

"Get outta here."

"A buck-friggin'-eighty, brother. I was having a good night anyway and this husband and wife, I was serving their dessert, they were my last customers—they were all over my shit all night—I said, you know something, this is the last dessert I will serve in this restaurant. I told them why I was leaving and the guy gives me his card, he said, here, you'll probably be looking for a job when you get back. This guy's a restaurant owner and he hits me with the century on the way out. I said, sir, that is very generous of you. If I ever come back, I'll call you."

The girl Mark was on the phone with was Icy. A girl he met playing pool at Roland's one night in the Bronx, a beautiful Puerto Rican girl from that neighborhood. In the short time that they knew each other they would play some more pool, listen to each other's favorite music and log some serious hours parked in the Green Regal, outside Icy's family's apartment under the elevated subway. Icy was upset about not being able to see Mark before he left. Between taking the ride down to say goodbye (which consisted of a pain-in-the-ass drive into the Bronx, then finding a place to park, which wouldn't be safe, dealing with Icy's family and her three-year-old son), or just calling her to say goodbye, Mark chose the phone call.

He spoke in quiet, apologetic tones, trying to explain that he still had so much to do. There was a lot of silence on his end as she was realizing that ultimately he just didn't want to see her. When they finally hung up, Mark sat on the bed in his room in his stepfather's house for a long moment and got uncharacteristically melancholy. From the living room came the sound of his mother watching TV. He put his headphones on and, in the dark, listened to Red Ryder's "Lunatic Fringe."

Holly was a year older than I was. She was heading off to finish up her first year at a SUNY, upstate in Cortland, while I was going to be traveling the country for an indefinite amount of time. Our goodbye lasted into the morning. We wanted to wrap it up quickly, with the least amount of sadness possible, but that *wasn't* possible. It wasn't a breakup; we loved each other, and that, of course, made it worse. We were in her mother's kitchen as the sun was coming up, one of her hands grabbing my shoulder, the other wiping her eyes with a paper towel; occasionally she tilted her head to the stairs to hear if her parents were waking up. I had so many thoughts in that moment when I walked out of her parents' house; things I was trying to comfort myself with.

"Jump and the net will appear." "God won't give you anything you can't handle." Nothing worked. We were two teenagers leaving someone we loved, it hurt hard, but there was nothing to be done about it and it sucked.

THE NIGHT WE left, Mark and Benny came to pick me up.

Mark was in the driver's seat and Benny was shotgun. After all my stuff was in, I sat in the captain's chair behind them. When the only thing left to do was drive, there was a pause. It was not expected and it lasted longer than any of us wanted it to. Benny broke it.

"I have to say one thing before we go. I feel like this trip is yours and I'm just along for the ride."

Another unwelcome pause.

I said, "B, I think that could be nerves. I don't think that only two of us *could* do this. It sounds like nerves."

He took a long moment to consider if that was true, then asked Mark, "What do you think?"

"I don't want to do this without you."

"You know what? You're right," Benny said. "You're right. You guys feel OK?"

"Yeah."

"Yeah."

"Forget it. I'm an idiot, let's go."

WE DROVE THROUGH the night. Our first stop was Hilton Head Island, South Carolina. It had ocean and it was warm even in January. So we stopped. We found a place to park overnight, which meant we found a place to sleep. After a few days we thought maybe we should move on, but why leave the beach? We were just getting used to the South. People were easier to talk to there. Not all of them, but some of them would actually look at you and smile when you passed them on the street. Some of them said hello. *Strangers said hello?* In Yonkers it was January and snowing, and the bridge was covered with it. A month ago we were sitting in a classroom waiting for a bell to ring. Now we were on the beach in South fucking Carolina with strangers waving to us. For the most part, people seemed to be genuinely intrigued with what we were doing. This, in turn, made us friendlier. It was easier to be interested in other people because now we were sure there was something special about us. We had something to offer.

We even found a place to play pool. Well . . . Benny found it. He disappeared one day when Mark and I were jogging on the beach, came back just before dark and said, "Fellas, grab your sticks." He'd discovered a severely run-down bar called the Sea Hog. The pool table looked like it had been the napping place for the countless Marines who'd stopped at Hilton Head on their way from Parris Island to Korea. The present clientele would happily talk about those days, if they could only remember them. The bartender's name was Grogan and the upside was that there was never a wait to get on the table.

Walking over to the Sea Hog one night, we passed an ice cream parlor and Mark noticed a girl working there whom he needed to speak with. He stopped dead in his tracks. Then, "Anybody want anything?"

"No, we're fine." We were smirking.

Mark said, "What? I just want an ice cream cone."

Benny and I sat on the bench outside and watched through the window. Mark talked, the girl laughed, next thing we knew, she was writing something down on a piece of paper, handing it to him. Benny smiled at me. "Huh. Check out southern hospitality over there."

Mark came out with his ice cream cone. "You guys wanna stay here for a couple weeks?"

The girl's name was Samantha. She had taken to Mark's story and the way he told it. As it turned out, Samantha had a friend who was trying to rent out a condo for two weeks while he was out of town. The condo had one bedroom, plenty of floor space, was within walking distance of the beach and would cost us each $150. This had all the earmarks of a situation that could potentially kick a lot of ass.

Benny said, "Fuckin' guy goes to get a pop rocket, comes back with a girlfriend and an apartment."

Mark said, smiling, "She has a boyfriend."

"Who is about to find out he doesn't have a girlfriend anymore."

Samantha was a professional wanderer who'd lived in six states from the age of eighteen to the age of twenty-four. She'd moved to Hilton Head Island about a year earlier with her boyfriend and they got a place together. He was a painter, and he was "artsy." We weren't quite sure what that meant, beyond the fact (which Samantha explained) that he didn't like to go out and party. Getting wind of that, Mark suggested that maybe she should go out with him for a night. Samantha told him she couldn't because of her boyfriend. Mark said, "He's not invited." When that didn't work, he said, "You bring a friend, I bring my fellas, we'll all go out together, no big deal."

So, Samantha produced her friend Karen. And the two of them took us to the only hot spot on the island—PJ's. It was a huge place, with waitress service at the tables and a dance floor. We drank Corona. With lime. Truly a step up from drinking cans of Coors Light on The Bridge. Of course, we were underage, but so was the waitress and, come on, we could do anything. We were the guys from New York who dropped out of high school to go to South Carolina and hang out in the hot bar with the beautiful local girls.

Samantha danced with Mark and I danced with Karen. Every so often we would look back to Benny sitting at the table and try to wave him up. He didn't come. Mark finally went over to the table, grabbed Benny's earlobe and asked him why he wasn't dancing. Benny slapped Mark's hand away hard enough to be serious and said, "Because I don't want to."

It happened that night that Mark and Samantha and I wound up sleeping at Karen's place. Benny headed home alone. The next morning, Samantha returned to her place and Mark and I, on no sleep, went back to our condo. On the way there, Mark asked me if he was a home wrecker.

We walked into the living room and heard Benny on the phone.

"Call Uncle Gino. He'll bring them over. Yeah, he will, but you gotta come down and unlock the door for him. . . . Yeah. Look in the . . . it should be in the book near . . . Don't worry about it, I'll call him. *Statti zitta, statti zitta,* I'll call. I'll call him today. I'll tell him to come over about three o'clock. I know what you need. . . . It's just groceries, Ma. I'm not the only person who can carry groceries. OK? Yes, it's OK. OK? All right. I will, OK? All right, Ma, I'm gonna go now. . . . I'm gonna go, but I'll call you soon. OK? OK, I love you. OK, 'bye."

Benny hung up. Looking right at Mark: "You juice her ringhole?"

Mark tried not to laugh. "Come on, B."

Then Benny looked at me.

"What?" I said.

"You pump 'er in the dumper?"

"No, Benny. I did not pump her in the dumper."

"No?"

"No."

Looking at Mark again: "What about this fuckin' guy? How'd he do?"

Mark walked into the bedroom.

Benny said to the closed door, "I'm glad you had a good night."

THE NEXT TIME we decided to go to PJ's, Benny didn't come with us. He opted for the Sea Hog.

Mark said, "Why don't we just play pool early, then we'll all go to PJ's and meet the girls."

"I don't want to go to PJ's."

"We came to South Carolina to play pool?"

I was deciding to stay out of this one.

"There's no big deal about what I wanna do. You're just making it that way. Now get off."

"Don't get bent," Mark said, sounding a little more than bent himself. "I just figured we could all go."

"You didn't figure that I don't want to go."

IT ONLY TOOK a few days for an intensity to develop between Mark and Samantha. She took to spending a lot of time with us. One night, the four of us were on the beach watching the sun go down. It started to feel a bit romantic, so Mark nudged Samantha and with a jerk of his head asked her if she wanted to take off.

"We're going for a walk."

I said, "See ya later."

I remember being captured by a simple happiness for them as they walked off. For him, mostly. A few months ago I was trying to talk him out of joining the Marines, for Christ's sake, and there he was arm in arm with a gorgeous (and I'm not just throwing that word on her) southern girl, listening to the waves, watching her get more beautiful in moonlight. We were miles away from home. Anyone could have seen them and said, "Oh, happy couple," or some such shit, but they wouldn't really have known how happy Mark was, or why.

When they were out of earshot, Benny, with his patent disgusted headshake, said, "Fuckin' guy."

"Come on, she's cool."

"I knew this was gonna happen. I know she's cool, but I knew this was gonna happen."

"Let's do some push-ups."

"Get off me."

"Don't be a pansy, do some push-ups with me."

He got up, mumbling again, "Fuckin' guy."

At that moment, Benny was mad enough to do forty-eight push-ups. When he got to about forty, I got all Vince Lombardi on his ass. "Go, B, go! Come on, you wanna be huge? Nine more, you limp-dick sissy! Come on, go, B! Forty-six, forty-seven! Come on, come on, come on, forty-eight! Come ooooon!"

He hit the sand. "AH, FUUUUCK!"

He was glowing and laughed half his ass off. "I had it. I almost had it, I almost hit fucking fifty, brother!"

"I told you, you lazy ass." I was mocking him, *"I can only do ten."*

He could barely talk, he was smiling so hard. "Fuck you, man, fuck you."

With both hands he gripped my forearm like an eagle, which was all he could do to stop himself from hugging me. A woman was going by with her little dog. The dog sensed Benny's adrenaline and started jumping all over him. The thing could barely reach his waist but kept biting at him and falling on its back, rolling all over the sand. They made their way down to the edge of the water, Benny and the dog, the woman letting it all happen. Benny laughed the second half of his ass off at the dog and at his own accomplishment. It was enough to make him enjoy the sunset again. To enjoy this trip again. To say fuck you to everyone back home again. To feel like no one we ever knew before would ever have made it to such a place. Then Mark and Samantha walked back toward us. On his way past me, Mark said affectionately, "Listen to his laugh."

Benny caught sight of the two of them and waited till they were way down the beach before he came back up from the water. The dog and its owner had gone. Benny sat next to me in the sand, breathing heavily through his nose. He shook his head at the sun.

"Fuckin' guy."

MARK, SAMANTHA, KAREN and myself became regulars at PJ's. Benny became a regular at the Sea Hog. And it wasn't just that he

had stopped going out with us at night; Benny also stopped going
to the beach with us. He said he was northern Italian and liable
to burn. Anyway, he didn't like to swim. He also started to feel
bad about not having a job. He had taken jobs in restaurants
since he was twelve and drifting seemed to be interfering with
his work ethic. Mark and I weren't even considering employ-
ment. On top of this, Mark and Benny started to fight.

One thing we didn't expect on this trip was that we would
come up against each other. It was supposed to be an "us against
them" situation. We were supposed to be out there saving each
other's lives or something like that. But things happen between
people that maybe they can't stop. Living on the same block for
eighteen years was OK, but the same condo for two weeks wasn't
turning out so hot for Benny and Mark.

It was a Saturday night and Samantha and Karen had invited a
few more of their friends out with us. Samantha's boyfriend was
still home being artsy, which was convenient for Mark. Benny
was at the Sea Hog again. This was feeling very wrong to me.
This was the fourth night we hadn't spent together. Of course,
Benny was free to do what he wanted. Nobody was supposed to
be making anybody do what he didn't want to do on this trip, but
still this was feeling wrong. I told Mark that I was going to the
Sea Hog to try and get Benny.

When I walked in, Benny was at the pool table. He was playing
one of the locals and the whole bar seemed to be watching.
Between shots, Benny looked back at Grogan, the bartender, and
signaled that he needed another beer. A customer at the bar said,
"That one's on me, Grogan."

Benny said, "Check out Jimmy Rockefeller over there.
Thanks, James. This one's for you. Four in the side."

He made the shot. It was a really nice shot, too. People tapped
their glasses on the bar as a compliment. I was not expecting
Benny to be so happy. But then I realized, this was a neighborhood bar and Benny was a neighborhood guy. Even on a tiny
island off the coast of South Carolina, where tourists go to play

golf and rich people build summer homes, where there is hardly any opportunity for a neighborhood to exist, Benny had found one. He'd found it in a skanky, bleak, washed-up bar, but it probably didn't seem bleak to its inhabitants. It didn't seem that way to Benny, either. He knew he somehow fit in.

Neighborhood guys—the real ones—are always in demand. Whatever they sell (which is usually authenticity and comfort), they sell more of it than the other guy. Wherever there's a crowd, the bulk of it huddles around them. Like the heads of the old-time immigrant New York City neighborhoods, they know every crack in the sidewalk and every store owner around. Benny was from Yonkers—a fertile patch of land that had cultivated masses of this kind. Suddenly I could see what a master Benny was at being that guy. And, right then, in the Sea Hog, as the four ball was sunk, I also thought I saw Benny Colangelo emanating his future. A future of work, neighborhood, family and the beautiful poetry of routine.

I said, "Nice shot, B."

He looked up. "Whooooa. Ladies and gentlemen, we are in the presence of greatness. The man who taught me all I know about felt and chalk, hailing from Yonkers, New York—the master of disaster—Mr. Joseph Frascone!"

As his new friends clapped, I was hoping he didn't mean what I thought he meant by "master of disaster."

I went over to him and spoke quietly. "Benny, when you're done wiping the table with this guy, why don't you come have a drink with me."

We didn't make a big deal about our entrance when we got to PJ's. I introduced him to Samantha's friends. Benny sat down at our table and said, "Who's our waitress?"

Mark didn't say much to him but was clearly happy he had come. A song started that got Samantha out of her chair. "This is my kind of funk." She killed the rest of her beer and took Benny by both hands and led him to the dance floor. She led, but made it look as if she were following. She was going easy with him and nodding to him as he was starting to follow the moves she was making. Then he started to anticipate them. Mark, Karen and I were clapping and screaming his name. Then, out of nowhere, Benny started to work the whole floor. Throwing Samantha around with the clumsiest grace we ever saw. Yeah, he almost knocked her over a few times, but he was laughing like a Girl Scout on good hashish, not giving a shit what he looked like or who was watching. He was laughing at himself, laughing at the guy who wouldn't dance a few nights ago.

At one point, he stepped on the back of some girl's heel and said, "I'm sorry, I'm from New York!" She shouted something back and he said, "I can't hear you, I'm from New York!" By now, the whole floor had made a circle for them (but really for Benny). The crowd was keeping the rhythm for them with their hands. Benny was now a street act and everyone was happily throwing him their last bits of change.

When the song was over, the happy couple came back to the table and we greeted Benny as if he were the go-ahead run crossing home plate in game seven. Then the bouncers came and asked us for ID.

As we walked through the parking lot, Mark kept looking back at the bar.

Benny was yelling, "Fuck you, assholes. All of a sudden they want ID from us? You guys were their best customers for weeks and now they kick us out? Bullshit, this is a fucked-up bar, fuck 'em, Markie."

Benny was psyched. Psyched he'd danced, psyched to be with his fellas, and psyched to get thrown out of a bar he never wanted to go back to again anyhow. But Mark was clearly miserable; Samantha wasn't following him out. We all got into the van and sat there for a moment.

Benny said, "That was fucked up. Those guys were fucked up."

I said, "I'll be right back."

Mark asked, "Where you going?"

"I'll be right back."

I got to the bouncer at the door. "Where you going?"

"Listen, my friend in there has my wallet. Could I just go in and get it?"

"Have your friend come out here."

This guy was funny.

"How can I do that?"

He said nothing. I guess he hadn't thought that far ahead.

"Listen," I said, "if I had anything to give you to hold until I came back out, I would give it to you, but my friend has my wallet in her pocketbook and I don't know when I'll be seeing her again. Could you please just let me in to get it? I'll be out in two minutes. If not, I owe you fifty bucks?"

"Two minutes."

"Thank you."

I grabbed Samantha by her shoulder and turned her to face me. She was startled for a second.

"Hi."

"Listen, I've known Mark for a long time and I've never seen him like this, so why don't you get your pocketbook, wave good-bye to your friends and come outside with me."

Going past the bouncer, I looked at my wrist for a watch that didn't exist. "How'd I do?"

Eyeing the blonde on my arm: "Looks like you did good."

Mark and Benny were leaning on the van. Mark walked toward Samantha and me and met her with a hug. He looked at me over Samantha's shoulder and mouthed the words, *Thank you*. Benny rested against the van, his arms folded over his chest. Of course Mark would hook up with something like this so fast, and of course I would get back into that bar to bring her out of there. Of course. The hug lasted a long time and Benny kept shaking his head.

When we got back to the condo, Mark and Samantha disappeared into the bedroom. I was in the bathroom brushing my teeth and Benny walked in, grabbed his toothbrush. He looked in the mirror at the arm he was brushing with. He touched his tricep to mark the effect of the push-ups. Then he got on his toes, turned his profile to get a better look at his chest. He caught my eyes and looked away with fast embarrassment, then rinsed out his mouth.

I said, "You're a kick-ass motherfucker."

He looked at his own eyes in the mirror for a second, then put his toothbrush back in its holder.

"Yeah, right."

THE NEXT MORNING, sometime after Samantha had tiptoed out of our condo, back to her own apartment, Benny was in his boxer shorts, making omelets for us. Mark walked by him bleary-eyed and said, "Nice pants."

"Thanks, ya fuck. Get the ketchup out."

Mark went to the refrigerator. Benny didn't take his eyes off him. It was like he was trying to read something Mark had printed on him. I sat down and we ate in silence for a little while.

Then Benny put down his fork. "All right. I gotta say something."

Mark said, "Go 'head."

There was a pause that didn't sound good.

Benny said, "So, listen . . . Well, where else do you guys wanna go?"

"I don't know," Mark said. "We eventually wanna go to California, right?"

I said, "Yeah."

"So, maybe Atlanta next. I don't know."

"Atlanta?" Benny said, as if he had tasted something he didn't like.

"Maybe. Why?"

"I don't know if I wanna go there."

"We could go to Memphis or Florida, it doesn't matter," Mark continued. "We could go anywhere."

Benny became insistent. "Well, tell me where."

"Why?"

"Because I wanna know."

"What difference does it make?"

I was hearing something in Benny's voice that Mark wasn't hearing yet. I said, "B?"

"What?"

"What did you want to say?"

Mark was glad the conversation was about to start over. "Yeah, what'd you wanna say?"

"I'm not sure I wanna go."

"Go where?" Mark asked.

"I think I wanna go somewhere else."

"Benny, what the fuck are you talking about?"

"I think I might wanna go back."

Mark lost all interest in his breakfast. "*What?*"

"I wanna go back."

"Why?"

"Because I just do."

"Why the fuck *do* you?"

"I do."

I decided to let the two of them finish this.

Mark, now shouting: "And what the fuck do you want to go back *for?*"

"Listen, how long do you think you can do this? You guys will eventually go back, too. I feel like I got no ground out here. I gotta ground myself. And maybe you guys are different. I just need to get some footing."

"What is there to sink your feet into back home? We tried that for the whole time we lived there, and it didn't work. It doesn't fuckin' work."

"It's different now."

"How so?"

"It's just different, Mark."

"Benny, if you want to leave the island now, we'll go. We can leave here today. We can do whatever the fuck we want out here. That's the whole point!"

"If we can do whatever the fuck we want, why can't I go back?"

"I mean, you could, but what the fuck? Nothing has changed there."

"You don't know that."

Mark couldn't counter this. Benny was right, Mark didn't know what Benny's relationship to the scenery was now going to be. I didn't, either, but Benny seemed to know.

"What'll you do?"

"Graduate high school, to start."

Now, that did it. "AND THEN WHAT?"

Benny was not going to fight with him and said so by giving Mark a cold stare. Mark got up from the table and started pacing the living room.

Benny continued, calmly, "All of a sudden, you're on my shit for doing what I want to do. I thought that was the whole point of this, to do whatever we wanted to do. Isn't that right?"

"You're doin' what we said we would never do."

"I could do whatever I want. I could go wherever I want so, I think I wanna go to Italy, all right? You think I'm gonna spend every day at home? Maybe I'm gonna take the money from my part of the van and go to Italy. Or somewhere."

"Benny, we don't have the friggn' money now. We have the van now."

"So, I'll wait for it."

"You know, I don't fuckin' . . ."

Benny jumped in while Mark was looking for the words. "What? What? Say it."

Mark started to sound defeated. "I don't fucking believe this."

"And I don't fucking believe that you would give me shit about doing what I want to do."

"That's not what I mean."

"What do you mean, then?"

"Do what you want to do, all right? Do what you want. Of course you can do what you want. I just can't fucking believe . . . now *I* don't know what to do."

"I'm not trying to stop you. You guys should keep going."

Mark stopped pacing and looked down at the carpet.

"Markie, I'm sorry. OK? I'm sorry. But, you guys should do it. You guys should keep goin'. I'm not comin'."

I DON'T KNOW what the thing was that allowed Mark Zadotti and Benny Colangelo to be born on the same block, or to throw the same eggs at the same cars on the same Halloween nights. I don't know what allowed them to hang out on the same bridge, or what let them drop out of the same high school. I don't know what it was. I do know there was a moment in their lives when they found themselves sitting in a 1980 green Ford van in Hilton Head Island, South Carolina, in front of an anonymous man's condo, ending—after two weeks—a cross-country trip they had planned for months. A trip that was supposed to have lasted an indefinite amount of time.

I was sitting right behind them in the captain's chair. I saw Benny take his stereo out of the Benzi-box, and I saw Mark stop himself from crying. They were trying to make the best of it. They were desperately trying to leave without a bad feeling toward each other. They were trying to convince themselves that this was OK. Benny was trying to convince Mark that he honestly *was* happier going back alone while Mark and I continued with the van.

Mark asked, "You gonna take a bus back to Yonkers?"

"Yeah."

"Where you going in Italy?"

Benny said, "What?"

"Italy, Benny. You said—"

"Oh, yeah, I probably got family there. I'll go where they are. Maybe. What are you guys gonna do?"

Mark sighed. He sounded like an adult. "I'm gonna go for a ride. I'll be back in a little while."

I got out of the van with Benny and on the walk into the condo I started to think about all the people I didn't know anymore. I started to think about all the people I might have to leave as time went on. What would my relationship with these guys be in a few years? What was going to happen to us? I had just left Holly. Would we be together again? I had no answers and it didn't seem to matter. Benny decided he wanted to cut out and Mark couldn't stop him. And if Mark couldn't stop him, I knew I didn't have a chance.

I was hoping this was a family thing. By which I mean this: I was hoping Benny could bring himself to leave us only because he knew at some point we would all be back together. Maybe this was just one moment of many that hung on the string that would always connect us.

I sat on the couch, Benny sat on a chair with the stereo still in his hands. I asked him if he was OK and he just shrugged. We sat there for a long time in silence.

Then he put the stereo on the coffee table, picked up the phone, dialed and started pacing back and forth.

"Ma? Hello, Ma? Ma? It's me, Ma. . . . Yeah, it's Benny, of course it's Benny. . . . What happened? You OK? Were you sleeping? You don't sound good. I woke you up? . . . Of course I'm safe. Whaddaya mean? I just called you yesterday—what's gonna happen to me in one day? . . . But don't be scared, Ma, because everything's OK . . . OK? . . . You sure? . . . No, I'm still in South Carolina. . . . It's still warm enough to swim. We're only a few blocks from it. . . . From the beach. It's beautiful here. No, everything's fine, Ma. Everything is good. We're fine, we're fine. . . . He's good, Markie's doin' good. Um, so . . . Uncle Gino shovel the sidewalk? He didn't? Don't worry, I'll call him. . . . Hey, Ma?"

He stopped pacing, turned his back to me and looked out the sliding glass door.

"Remember how I told you that I don't like to dance? . . . Well, I danced, Ma. We all went out, me and Joe and Mark and these really nice girls that we met from here, we all went out and I danced. . . ."

I got up from the couch, went into the next room and let him continue alone.

Frank Gianguzzi had a thick crop of blond, northern Italian hair and blue-gray eyes—two homicides about to happen. He was very proud of his heritage, and what little Italian he knew, he spoke very often. Frank's term of endearment for everyone was "coog," from the Italian *cugino*, meaning "cousin." He also coined variations on that word. He might have called you coog-o, coogini, coogette (if you were a girl), coogie-coog, coolie-coog, coog a'bell, coog a'brut, coog a'pants, etc. Everyone was Frank's cousin. Except if he didn't like you, then you were de-cooged.

Frank had lifted many weights by the time he was twenty-one, and to declare this, he wore the sleeves of his shirt rolled up over his biceps. Every night before work he would ask me to do this for him so the crease would be perfect. He'd stick his arm in front of me and say, "Coog, gimme a twist-assist." If Frank had women at the bar, they would always have their drink served with a flexed arm. Danny and I would watch him deliver drinks like that over and over and it never got old. "There he goes . . . and there's the arm."

A few years before we worked at the bar together, Frank was a coffee boy at a local Sons of Italy Club, where his father was a member. One night there was a card game going on with the members and a local parish priest. During the game one guy exchanged what Frank considered disrespectful and unpleasant words with the priest. Frank told the guy to watch his mouth, the guy told Frank to remember who he was, and next thing anyone knew, three Sons of Italy were trying to pull Frank off a man three times his age. With one Son on each arm, he couldn't swing; so at sixteen years old Frank Gianguzzi started spitting at a forty-five-year-old wise guy. They threw Frank into a back room. This was a room the Sons of Italy had reserved for just such occasions—the in-case-shit-goes-wrong room. It had no windows and a metal door that locked from the outside. After about an hour, when the noise in the room started to die down, Frank's father was called to come get him. When Mr. Gianguzzi showed up, he made sure Frank did two things. First, pay for the metal door he'd just dented—second, find a job somewhere else.

One time I saw Frank fight a guy because the guy asked him what Italian pussy tasted like. "Like your pants that I made you shit in then shoved down your throat. Any other questions? Asshole?" What the other guy didn't understand was that that wasn't a real question. That was a warning for the guy to stop talking and scram. But the guy actually answered, "No," which left Frank with no choice.

DANNY RYAN GREW up in bars. Chances are, he was conceived in one. Danny was born between three older brothers and one younger sister. His father Pat owned a bar called the Side Car Saloon on McLean Avenue in Yonkers. Danny's mother Irene used to cocktail-waitress there a few nights a week even during all five of her pregnancies. When the kids were born, none of the Ryans' friends came to their house; instead there was a special day reserved at the Side Car for the unveiling of the newborn. Friends would gather around the latest Ryan with Bloody Marys in their hands and point out the features of the child's face and body as if he were a new pool table or jukebox.

Pat and Irene held all the important family functions at the Side Car: the kids' first birthdays, fifth birthdays, christenings— even after-funeral gatherings. They only held one of those. It was for Danny's younger sister, Wendy.

Wendy and I were the same age and I'd known her all through elementary school. In the third grade I tried to flirt with her by throwing an eraser at her while the teacher wasn't looking. I accidentally hit her in the eye and spent the whole lunch hour writing an apology note, which I gave to her in secret. Wendy was diagnosed with Hodgkin's disease at twelve and the illness took her within a year. During that year-long fight, Irene spent many months in the hospital, on a cot, sleeping next to her. By the time Wendy fell sick, the Ryan boys were considered grown—which is to say, their parents stopped worrying about them. So, with Irene at the hospital and Pat at the Side Car every night, the boys were left to themselves. All of Danny's brothers still lived in their parents' house, but each had his own life, with cars and jobs and girlfriends. Danny was only fourteen at the time and had to get rides from his brothers to go visit Wendy. Danny didn't learn to cook, clean and keep up the house as much as he learned to walk the two miles down to the Side Car and eat a plate of chicken wings for dinner or ask his father for some money for pizza. That was the year Danny was in the ninth grade; the same year he was asked to leave school one day when the school nurse found a tick in his hair.

After her daughter Wendy passed away, Irene integrated herself back into the house the way an orphan might ingratiate herself into her new foster home—without the enthusiasm or sense of entitlement it would take to try and change the way the household had been operating without her. Anyway, the Ryans' house was never their nucleus or source of pride. The Side Car was their consecrated space. And two years after Wendy's death, they lost that too.

Everyone saw it coming. Grief and alcohol teamed up inside Pat Ryan and bare-knuckled him to the ground. And on his way down, Pat took the Side Car Saloon with him. After a year of fighting for her youngest child and only daughter, Irene didn't have it in her to continue fighting for the preservation of her husband's well-being. During Danny's last two years of high school, the only money brought into the Ryan household was what the three eldest boys made. There was very little else the family had to live off of.

I MET HER one night at work. Frank, Danny and I were behind the bar. This was the same night I took that ride with Danny. It was the Wednesday before Thanksgiving, traditionally a big evening out. The only thing anyone was required to do the next day was wake up late and eat. I was nineteen. She walked up to the bar and asked me if I was even old enough to tend bar. I asked if she was afraid she might be attracted to me. She snapped back at me and in so many words told me to cut the shit. "You're right," I said, "I'm sorry. The holidays put me in a wise-ass mood. I'm sorry." I put a cardboard coaster down in front of her. "Now what can I get you, ma'am?"

"Tanqueray and tonic. Kid."

"Wow, an actual great-looking older woman who's not afraid to bust my chops. Cool. You want lime in that?"

"Don't make me feel older than I already do when I come back here."

"Back here? From where?"

"The city."

"Wow, an actual great-looking older woman *from Manhattan* who's not afraid to bust my chops. This is gonna be a great night." That one she let me get away with. I said, "You came to see your family for Thanksgiving?"

"Yup."

"And you came to this place by yourself?"

"God, no. My little sister's at a table over there. With her new boyfriend and one of his friends."

"Got set up, did you?"

"It's not like that, believe me. Although he thinks it is."

"So hang out with me for a while. If after five minutes I turn out to be another bridge-and-tunnel jerk, you could always go back to your sister and your blind date. No harm done."

"Right. No harm done," she said. "And yes, I would like a lime in that. What about these other two guys?" she said. "They look barely old enough to drink, too."

"Shhh. They both are. And legally all you need is one person over twenty-one and the rest have to be eighteen or older. Or that's what Frank keeps telling me."

"Which one's Frank?"

"The guy with the blond hair."

"Frankie muscles?"

"That's not what we call him."

"Is he your buddy?" she asked.

"Yeah."

"I remember guys like Frank."

"Fondly?"

"Brutally."

"What do you remember about guys like me?"

"I'm not sure."

WHEN DANNY'S FATHER Pat walked into our bar that night, Frank and I looked at each other, then I looked over to Danny, who had already decided not to greet his dad.

Frank said, "You wanna take Pat or should I?"

"No, I got him," I said.

"Hey, Coog. That brunette you're talkin' to? I would eat her ass through a screen door."

"Step off," I said.

"Little Joey going for the older ladies."

I went over to Danny's dad.

"Hi, Pat."

"Joseph."

He clamped my hand between both of his. He was having trouble focusing on my eyes.

"How you doin'?" I said.

"I'm good as good can be."

I thought of saying Happy Thanksgiving. I thought of asking him how Irene was and what they were doing tomorrow. But instead I asked him what he wanted to drink. He put his hands to his chest and said he needed something good for the heart.

I went over to Danny and asked if he wanted to start a tab for his father.

"No," he said. "He pays as he goes."

"OK."

As I walked away, Danny said, "What's he drinking?"

I tried to answer as if Pat ordered the most harmless liquid we carried. "Beer." But Danny's disgust just grew.

THE PLACE WAS starting to fill up. Most of the tables were taken and the bar was at least one deep all around. Danny was staying away from his dad, which limited his working space for a while. By the time I caught up with all the drinks that needed to be poured, I saw that Frank was throwing his rap on the girl I'd been talking to. But that was allowed. You didn't have dibs on the beautiful girl just because you got to her first. When Frank finally walked away from her, I stepped in and pushed a rag over her area, which wasn't dirty to begin with. She said to me, "Frank's a real tough guy, huh?"

"No, he's just Italian."

"Just like you."

"Is it that obvious?"

"Maybe not to everyone."

"Listen, Frank's a great guy. I've known him since I'm five. He's fuckin' funny, too. Always has been. I'll tell you a funny story about Frank. I was in the first grade and he was in third, OK? And we were outside our elementary school, drawing in the mud with sticks. It was before school started, before the bell rang? And this other little kid walked over, his name was Gregory, he had this okeydokey-let's-be-friends look on his face. Right? He squats down next to Frank and says, 'Hey, whacha doin'?' Frank looks up at him—we're, like, seven or eight years old, right? He looks up at him with this squint and without even missing a beat he says, 'We're playin' tic-tac-toe on your mother's ass.' "

I was laughing at my own story, but she wasn't.

I said, "Third grade. Do you believe that?"

She had a vague smile on her lips.

"That's a fuckin' riot, isn't it?" I stopped laughing. "You don't think that's funny?"

"Yeah, it's funny." She was being very matter-of-factual. "It'd be funnier if it wasn't so tragic. Frank's telling the same kind of jokes now that he was when he was seven. Chances are he'll be doing that when he's sixty."

"You think?"

She said, "Tic-tac-toe is not exactly the kind of game you can get better at. You know? Whoever goes first, wins. How many asses do you have to scribble on to realize that?"

Then, just as things were starting to go so well between us, I got hit in the side of the head with a lemon wedge. It was Danny trying to get my attention.

I said, "Excuse me."

I walked over to Danny, who was at the tap pouring a pitcher. "What's up?"

"Don't serve my father after that one."

"OK. But I'd rather not be the one to cut him off, you know?"

"Just ignore him or whatever, but don't give him another one. Tell Frank."

"All right."

"SO YOU KNOW I'm Italian," I said to her. "What's your background?"

"I am . . . ready for this? Dutch, Irish, Spanish, German, but mostly Polish."

"I can see the Irish and maybe the Spanish thing, but, stare as I might at your beautiful black curly hair and sea-green eyes, it's hard for me to spot your Polish roots."

A beat passed.

"Let me ask you something." She was exasperated. "You have a girlfriend?"

"Not anymore."

"Did you screw it up?"

"Did *I* screw it up?"

"Yeah, did you?"

"Depends on who you ask."

"Did you cheat on her?"

"Um . . . technically?"

"Um . . . so, you did screw it up."

"Maybe."

"So why do you keep doing this thing you're doing?"

"What thing?"

"See how you're looking at me right now?"

"How?"

"You know what I mean. Tell me if I'm wrong, but you've developed a crush on me. Right?"

I denied nothing.

"But it's not so much because you actually like me. You want me to like you. You want *me* to develop a crush on *you*. Yes? Tell me if I'm wrong."

"You might not be."

"OK, so this girl? She really liked you?"

"Yeah."

"I mean, she *really* liked you. She fell in love with you, right?"

"Yes."

"And you wouldn't have had it any other way. Yes?"

"Whaddaya mean?"

"I mean, it was the same deal with her. You wanted her to be

CITY OF LIMERICK PUBLIC LIBRARY

floored by you. That was your intention. Am I right? Because when that's happening, that's when you feel good about yourself. You don't get together with someone unless they're gonna be absolutely nuts about you. You aggrandize yourself that way. You've been trying to do it to me since the moment I came up here. You're doing it right now."

She waited for my retort, which didn't come.

"You think it's an accident that you're already behind a bar at eighteen years old? This is the perfect place for you to do your thing."

"I'm nineteen. And this is not the perfect place for me. It's not like I'm going to be here forever."

"Where you gonna be, then?"

"I don't know. Maybe somewhere out West."

"You've been there?"

"Once. I drove cross-country once."

"Why'd you come back?"

"What?"

"Why'd you come back?"

I couldn't hold her gaze. I was looking at the bar, out the window, at my hands, at her hair, trying not to remember that trip, the two friends I went with and how our relationships didn't survive it. How humiliating our decision was to come back here and how hideously silent the ride home was. How that failure continued to annihilate me and, since then, how isolated I felt in this bereft fucking place.

"Listen," I said, "maybe we should slow down or start over."

"OK. I'm Leda."

"Joe."

We shook.

"Why'd you come back, Joe?"

And that was it. Fifteen minutes in this woman's presence and I was a sorry little teenager who used relationships to aggrandize himself, couldn't last a second with the city girl and had no idea why he was back in his hometown hurling beers.

"It's just that I can tell you're not happy here," she said.

"You might be right."

"Listen, I'm not trying to piss you off. I mean, you could tell me to mind my own business and I would."

"All right. But I don't wanna tell you that."

"One thing I know something about is being unhappy with where you are, Joe. Ask yourself why I seem to know so much about how love can be used as self-aggrandizement."

"Because plenty of guys have done it to you before?"

"Close."

THE BAR GOT packed. We turned the lights down and the music up. People were putting their beers on the jukebox and windowsill. Danny's father was talking to two girls half his age. Twice I passed him and pretended I didn't hear him call my name. The third time he reached his empty glass over the bar and hit me in the arm with it.

I said, "Listen, Pat, I don't know if it's a good idea."

"Oh, you're kiddin' me. You're kiddin' me. How long have you been workin' behind a bar, Joe?"

"Not as long as you, Pat."

"That's right. So how would you know if it's a good idea or not?"

I said, "Talk to Danny," and walked away.

I looked back and saw him pull an airplane bottle of Smirnoff out of his coat pocket, crack it open and take it down in one sip. Danny saw it happen too. He told me to cover for him and not to let his father leave the bar. He was calling him a cab and wasn't letting him drive home.

THE TIPS WERE coming in at the holiday rate. Other guys struck up conversations with Leda; but they didn't last very long. I had never seen anyone so comfortable and content sitting in a crowded bar by herself. This girl mystified me. No one had ever turned me inside out with such ease. And although it didn't feel great, I was dying to see what else she was going to show me about me.

"So Leda, what can one do about this self-aggrandizing condition?"

"Listen, I didn't mean to be harsh, Joe. Was I?"

"Probably not."

"Don't worry, because you probably don't snore or leave the bathroom messy. And no, I don't want to find out for sure, so don't ask."

"I wasn't going to."

We shared a laugh over that.

A guy had muscled his way to the bar and said, "Don't ask what?"

Leda turned around to him and said, "Hi, Paul."

Paul said, "So, what's up?

"A preposition."

"Oh, I like this one, she's sharp. Whussa matter, you don't like our table? Rather hang out with the bartender?"

I made myself busy washing clean glasses and pretended I wasn't listening.

"No," Leda said to him. "I've known this guy's family my whole life. His mother was my sixth-grade teacher. I couldn't believe I saw him here, I was just catching up." Then she yelled to me, "Small town, right, Joe?"

"Yeah," I yelled back.

Leda said, "I didn't mean to upset anyone, Paul."

"You kidding? The only time I get upset is if I lose money or my car gets dented."

"Well, good. I'm coming right over, let me just settle up."

"I got it, I got it." Paul slapped a twenty down.

"OK, I'll be right over."

Paul walked back to the table.

"My sister said, 'You're gonna love this guy. He's so sweet.' Did I mention how much I love my sister?"

"No."

"I do. I should probably get over there."

"So Leda, before you go, tell me, what's so great about the city?"

"The weather."

"Yeah, thank God for the weather. New York's the first place I go when I want some weather."

"No, I mean the weather's great because the city's personality changes when the weather does. We get that sexy humid heat in the summer. And I don't care where you are; nothing is as hot as a New York summer. A summer in Cairo isn't as hot as a New York summer. Then, when it snows, there's that insulated silence, that peace. And the rain? At night when it rains, it actually gets brighter because all the lights shine off the street. It's like walking on stained glass. And I don't even want to talk about the autumn."

"And that's the greatest part, huh?"

"Yes. That and you're never more than five blocks away from an Etta James song." Now she laughed at her own joke. "I'll tell you, though. Because I like you, I'll tell you the moment when I realized that I loved New York." She hiked herself up on the stool. "OK. You know sometimes when you get an itch on your foot and you can't scratch it because you're wearing shoes?"

"Yes. No clue as to where you're going with this, but yes."

"So you know the itch. About two years ago, I was walking down the street and a woman walking toward me stopped, bent down and through her boots was trying to scratch an itch. But she couldn't get to it. And she couldn't take her boot off because she's on the street. So she started to step on it with her other foot. And she's got that squinty look on her face like she can't stand it anymore. Right? So, just as I passed her I said, 'Don't you hate that?' and she laughed. That was it. I kept going and she kept going. An entire relationship based on us admitting one thing to each other: That we both have had itches we couldn't scratch. We'd both been in the same situation before. The relationship lasted about three seconds. But it was perfect. So perfect that now, two years later, it still exists. She's still with me and that moment is still with me. And those moments of recognition are where I want to live."

She leaned closer into me.

"In New York—at any given time or place—it feels like all you could possibly want exists right in front of you. All that you've ever wanted to know. It's right there for you. Does that answer your question?"

I was searching my insides for something that shifted or broke during her story. Something had. And Leda knew it.

"It's not where you're from, Joe. It's where you go." She got up from the stool to make her way to her sister's table, put her hand on Paul's twenty and pushed it closer to me. "Here," she said. "I made you some money tonight."

WHEN THE PLACE started to slow down, Danny finally went over to his dad, interrupted his conversation with the two young ladies and told him there was a cab waiting outside for him. That information inspired great discontent in Mr. Ryan. Soon, Danny was on the other side of the bar telling Pat that he didn't give a shit what he did as long as he didn't do it at this bar. Danny stood over his father's stool until he finally got up and made for the door.

Danny had his hand on his father's back when they walked out of the bar. Through the window, Frank and I were watching as Pat walked right to his own car and tried to unlock the driver's-side door. Danny knocked his arm away from the lock, twice. And then, keys in hand, Pat swung around and slapped his son across the face. Danny grabbed Pat by his lapels and cocked one fist back. In the millisecond of the swing, Danny thought differently of the fist and landed an open-hand shove into his father's chest. It was enough to slam Pat against his car and down to one knee. He came back up and lunged. Danny sidestepped it and threw a bear hug on him from behind and slammed him, stomach first, into the car door. Pat squirmed, but his arms were pinned to his sides. They looked like two animals that had been scraped off the street by a snowplow and packed against the side of the car.

By then a small crowd of customers had gathered by the window to watch. When Danny finally released his dad, they stood and faced each other, vapor shooting out of their mouths. With a finger pointed right between his father's eyes, Danny barked something with the direct and contained rage of a leashed dog. His father said nothing; just swayed slightly with one hand on the car to keep himself from falling.

When Danny came back into the bar, the crowd at the window pretended they hadn't been watching. They had their heads pointed down at their drinks, but their eyes were on him as he jumped back behind the bar.

If there was something to be said or done, it was not obvious to Frank or me; so we stayed quiet as Danny did two quick shots of Wild Turkey, said, "I'll be right back," and went downstairs. He did the shots in the same amount of time it took Mr. Ryan to get in his car, start it up and drive away.

DANNY EVENTUALLY CAME upstairs and went through the motions for the rest of the night without mentioning what had happened. Leda, and the people she was with, got up from their table and put their coats on. Leda left them, came over to me and grabbed both of my hands over the bar.

"It was an absolute pleasure," she said.

"For me, too."

We locked a smile on each other. I heard the cash register ring behind me. I wanted to jump over the bar and ask her if there was any possibility that she might take me to wherever it was she was going.

"You just gonna leave me here with these guys?"

"Will you take care, Joey?"

"Yeah."

She squeezed my hands once and hard, then turned toward the door.

IT WAS ABOUT two A.M. We had already brought the money down to the safe. Frank had four of his boys at the bar killing one more while they waited for him to walk out. They were planning to go to Katty's Korner, the local strip club. I was splitting up our tips and Frank was wiping down the last of the bar.

"Coog-O, you comin'?"

"Where?"

"To the Korner, you comin'?"

"Oh . . . nah."

"Why not?"

"Because it's Thanksgiving."

"Like it's a religious holiday? Who gives a shit? And you gotta watch *this* fucking guy." He pointed to one of his boys. "He always gets a kiss from one of them. Right, Mike? Mike!"

"What?"

"Don't the dancers always kiss you?"

"Yeah," Mike said. "I don't know what the hell, but those chicks are all into me. I'm like a miracle waitin' to happen in that place."

The other guys started to rouse him.

"That guy's a rabbit's foot," Frank said to me. "Come with us."

"No, I gotta—"

"Oh, I know where you're goin'. You're goin' to meet that one from tonight, with the curly hair."

"No, I'm not."

"You dog, you are, too."

"I'm not."

"Shut the fuck up. You get her number?"

"No."

"Bullshit."

"Stop it, I'm takin' a ride with Danny."

Frank nodded. "You goin' down?"

"Yeah."

I handed him his share of the tips. "Here."

"We break two?" he asked.

"We're a fin short."

"Uh, right, I'll take it."

DANNY DROVE SOUTH on I-87 and got off on 239th Street in the Bronx. He continued down White Plains Road, under the elevated train. At a stoplight five guys charged the car, holding nickel and dime bags of pot. Danny waved them off. I said, "Isn't that what you wanted?"

"That shit's dirt weed. I found a better place."

That's when it started to feel wrong to me.

I'd taken the ride with Danny plenty of times before and that's the spot where we always scored. He drove into an unfamiliar neighborhood. The streets were deserted. And no cars were stopping for red lights.

He pulled over next to a row of abandoned buildings. One of them had a red door with a dim light shining on it. "I'll be right out," he said. And took the keys with him. I watched him knock on the red door and it opened just enough for him to squeeze inside.

It was silent in the car. No engine idling, no radio, no wind cutting through a cracked window. I could only hear the heartbeat inside my head. Sitting there didn't seem smart. I felt if something was going to happen I wouldn't be able to see where it was coming from, so I got out.

The street was lined with abandoned buildings and the one Danny went in was the shortest of them all. It looked like a chipped tooth, neglected and decaying. The buildings had boards in the windows or no windows at all. This was the place where if you got killed no one would know about it for weeks.

The red door cracked open and Danny walked out.

"You get what you wanted?" I said.

"Yeah."

"Good. Can we get outta here?"

ON THE WAY back Danny did his standard eighty-five to ninety miles an hour while lighting a cigarette. With matches. He kept his eyes on the road with the eerie focus of a shark. Only then had I seen the welt under his right eye. Before I could ask him if he wanted to talk about the fact that he and his father almost beat the shit out of each other outside the bar tonight, he told me he needed gas and pulled into a station right along the highway. He got out of the car and said, "I gotta pee first."

A long while passed before Danny came out of the bathroom and started pumping the gas. Out of the window I saw he was swaying and his eyes were opening and closing. When I got out of the car I saw what was up.

Danny was holding the pump with one hand and there was blood dripping down his arm. Fuck. This guy made me take a ride with him to buy heroin. I felt like a true jerk. A true bridge-and-tunnel jerk. What the fuck did I come back here for? Only thing to do was make sure Danny wasn't behind the wheel for the rest of the way. I wasn't going to die driving back to Yonkers.

"You OK?" I asked.

He nodded his head slowly. The highway transfixed his dilated eyes. He fell deep into the rhythm of the passing cars and said, "Look at all these people goin' by." His words weren't directed at me; I just happened to be standing there when they dropped out of his mouth. He flicked his cigarette into the traffic and orange sparks shot out over the interstate. I had to convince him to let me drive the rest of the way home, but I didn't want to do that yet.

The gas pump clicked past nine dollars. The station attendant turned up the volume of his radio. To the right was where Danny and Frank and I lived. To the left was the skyline of New York City. I was staring right into its lights.

I tried to picture Leda sitting on a couch, alone in her apartment, but I had no idea what any of her stuff looked like.

I wasn't falling asleep next to a campfire, under the stars, with a horse named Stetson, but four-thirty A.M. on a Wednesday in New York City felt like the frontier to me. Bartenders and jazz musicians. The occasional nine-to-five guy who looks as if he'll fall to the sidewalk any second if a cab doesn't come and save him. Cleaning ladies outside of a bookstore taking a cigarette break, a minivan full of hookers with their daddy standing outside, keeping it safe for them, and firemen on the street telling jokes during a call. Some nights, my feet hurt so much from ten hours of tending bar that I wanted to limp out of my shoes and walk home in my socks, but I never took a cab. Seeing the wave of traffic lights changing down Ninth Avenue, the stark buildings just standing there, and the asphalt lying still, not saying a word . . . The silence outweighed the noise. It's what I imagine it would feel like to sneak into a museum after closing time. Only menacing.

It was about as cowboy as I could get. But it wasn't cowboy enough.

I knew there were bizarre perspectives on this world I'd never even heard of. And I wanted them. I wanted to do something audacious that would scare me witless. I wanted to be out of my mind with fear. Maybe some mystical sage could appear from an alley with an entourage of strange and eccentric creatures and send me off on a hero's journey.

If it seems like a stretch to say that this way of begging for an epiphany, these long walks home in the wee hours, led me to run drugs from Jamaica to America, then I'm very sorry.

But it did.

GIL Z CAME in once a week to deliver for my manager, Anthony. It took me about four months to realize that Anthony was calling him Gil Z. I thought he was saying Gilzie. I thought it was a term of endearment. Which didn't make sense, because Gil Z never struck me as the kind of guy people found endearing. As it turned out, the Z stood for a long Czechoslovakian-sounding last name that no one could pronounce. Ever. Too many consonants. Gil hung the Z after his first name like a sign outside the fence of his identity, which read:

NO ENTRY
PERPETRATORS
SHOT ON SIGHT

Gil Z had a tab that Anthony always signed for. Anthony could smoke an ounce of pot in a weekend, so that was his way of getting a discount.

It was simple. All I said was, "Gil, you looking for any new employees?"

He said, "You already have a job."

I said, "Maybe I'm bored."

Then he told me to meet him at Penn Bar on 31st and 8th.

SHE SAID, "I think you just feel like being a fuckin' maniac and you're bullshitting yourself into thinking it's gonna be something more than a sick fuck thing to do."

Her eyes were so dark I had to struggle to see where her pupils ended and her irises began. She was roughly six feet tall, tough, funny and from Brooklyn.

I said, "It's not a sick fuck thing to do."

"It's not a sick fuck thing?"

"No," I said. "I don't mean it's not a sick fuck thing. I mean the reasons why I'm doing it are not sick fuck reasons."

"You don't know why, you have no clue as to why you're doing it. You're like a little kid who gets bored of his toys too fast."

"Would you come on."

"Let me ask you something—"

"Don't I always?"

"Yes, you little wiseass, you do." She shot me a sneer. "Is going to jail part of this plan?"

"I'm not going to jail."

"And you know this how?"

I just kept her stare because I really didn't know. "Look, are you trying to talk me out of this?"

"Talk you out of it? What do I ever try to talk you out of? I don't even try to talk you out of going to some other girl's apartment at three A.M., when you're lucky enough to get invited in."

"It's only two-thirty."

"I know you're not missing my point. I just want you to see what it is you're getting into. What it is you're *truly* getting into."

"Well, you're right I don't know what I'm getting into. How can I? And neither do you. Not really."

She lay down with her head in my lap and rubbed her eyes.

"Look," she said. "Do what you have to do. Don't I always tell you that when it comes to fucked-up things you want to do?"

"Yes, you little wiseass. You do."

"I'LL TELL YOU what this is," said Gil Z. "You ever been in this line of work before?"

"Only on the buying end."

"Yeah, I know you bought before, but did you ever move or sell or grow?"

"No."

"Where you from?"

"Yonkers."

"Jesus Christ."

"Tell me about it."

"I'll give you a little background. I don't deal anything heavier than green. I move from here, from Canada, Europe and Jamaica. I get blueberry and bubble gum from Canada or Vermont, purple haze from Amsterdam, white rhino, thai, chocolate thai, no schwag, never schwag. No offense, but that's a whole different clientele and I'm not into that. What I have goes twenty for a gram, a hundred for five, and that's top-notch. If you go I'd be sending you for Jamaican red and gold. It's hydroponically grown, but it is not crystallized, therefore not particularly abundant in THC."

"Who's your contact over there?"

"He's a partner." He was smart to correct me. "Partner" made it sound like it was someone he trusted. "Andre. He's the only one you'll deal with. He's the grower and he packs it."

"How's it packed?"

"Compressed pellets wrapped in latex."

"How's that done?"

"In car engine parts, actually. He puts the buds in the shaft where the pistons pump and that's how they're compressed. I brought the parts over there myself. It took three years, seven trips. So the buds get compacted in the shaft of the engine. You get about one hundred pellets per pound. A pound is what I'd be asking you to bring back."

"What's the worst-case scenario?"

"Worst-case scenario? You get busted. If something happens in Jamaica, for enough of the profit they let you go and put you on the undesirable list, that's no problem. I know how to handle that. If something happens when you get back to New York, that might require the assistance of a lawyer. You don't have any priors, do you?"

"Not drug trafficking."

"What do you have?"

"A bullshit assault."

"You do time for it?"

"No."

"Forget it. Don't even worry about that. That doesn't mean shit to them."

I didn't know whether to believe that or not. But I wasn't about to say, *Really?*

I said, "You ever get busted?"

He stopped for a second. "Yeah, once."

He wasn't offering more than that, so I asked for it.

"What happened?"

"Someone tipped someone off."

"You do any time?"

"No."

"So, how did it go down?"

With a long inhalation he bought the time he needed to decide whether he was going to tell me about it or not.

"This was when we first started." It took him three tries to pull a cigarette out of its pack. He bounced it off the table a few times, put it in his mouth backward and didn't even notice.

"We used to form it in bricks and vacuum-pack it. It was the best way to get around the dogs. When there's no exchange of air molecules coming in and out of the brick, the dogs can't smell it. And I'd put it in the lining of my suitcase."

I was taking him to a place he didn't want to go. As he remembered it, his eyes darted around so fast and sharp I felt he could have sliced a Z right in my chest like a master swordsman.

"I got pulled right off the line at customs. Which they never do. They always look through your shit before they pull you aside. But they pulled me right off. And I didn't look like some UVM stoner punk or some hippie-trippy that they normally fuck with. I was in Armani head-to-toe with Louis Vuitton luggage and a yarmulke. No reason for them to fuck with me. And I knew I did everything right. They took me to this back room and this is how I know they got tipped off. A guy walked in with a handheld power drill and drilled right through the closed compartment of my suitcase where the bricks were. They just knew. They got me on a tip. That's why everybody swallows now."

Gil had his cigarette in and out of his mouth so many times that when he finally got around to lighting it, both sides of it were wet from his saliva.

"Anyone you send ever get busted?" I asked.

"No. The closest it ever came was when I sent this guy who was black, and that was my mistake. They took him into a room. Held him for four hours. They were in his face saying, 'We know you've got a pound of pot in your stomach right now!' And he had to sit there and hold it."

"What happened?"

"They couldn't detain him. They really didn't have anything on him even though they were right."

I was wondering how I would hold up under something like that.

"So," I said. "One hundred pellets per pound, huh?"

"About a hundred. Sometimes less, but never much more than that. It just feels like a big meal, nothing to it. It's really easy to set up if you want to do it. It just takes a few phone calls. You want to do it?"

"What's it pay?"

"Seven hundred. But that's only if you bring it back with you. The way I see it, it's a four-day vacation and one day's work."

"Yeah, sure, what the fuck."

"OK, my travel agent will be calling you, she'll set the whole thing up. Her name is Marci. Also, you should get a haircut and wear some nice clothes for the flight home. Look like a rich kid. They may smoke more than you, but they don't deal. Customs in New York is easy; just tell them you were at Club Med. And think of a good reason why you were in Ocho Rios alone for five days. That's all. Ever been to Jamaica?"

"No."

"It's really nice. Just be careful of the girls over there. Don't go divin' without a wet suit."

Simple.

I guess I wasn't such a hard sell. I'd get paid seven hundred dollars to hang out in Ocho Rios for five days. Airfare, hotel, food and all the Red Stripe I could drink was included. All I had to do is come back to New York with a pound of marijuana in my stomach. Perfect. It was exactly the terrifying vacation I was looking for.

"SEVEN HUNDRED DOLLARS?" she said. "That's it?"

"Yeah."

"You're getting played for a sucker. You know that?"

"Only from a business perspective."

"He's gonna make ten grand off what you're bringing back."

"Nine."

"Oh, I'm sorry, nine thousand dollars. And how many cents?"

"I'm not looking at this as a business venture."

"So what is it?"

"I just want the experience."

"You just want the experience."

"Yeah."

"And what experience do you want?"

"That's hard to explain."

"If your goombah friends from Yonkers could see you now."

She got up, lit a cigarette, opened the window and stood in front of it.

"So, you have plans for the rest of the night?"

"It's four A.M., what am I gonna do? Laundry? No, I have no plans."

"You gonna go home?"

"I thought I would stay here."

"If you wanna get laid, don't let me stop you."

"I would like to sleep over. If that's OK."

She blew some smoke out the window.

I said, "Please? Pretty please? Pretty please with Jamaican beef patties on top?"

"Take a shower first, you reek of Beefeater."

After the shower we got into bed, her back to my chest. I had my hand in her hair.

She said, "It's ironic, don't you think?"

"What is?"

"That you could be so clear about what you want out of dealing drugs, but you have no idea what you want from me."

"I want to sleep over."

"*Sometimes* you want to sleep over."

"True."

"When you have nowhere else to sleep. Some would say that's compartmentalizing."

"Some would say those psychological terms don't apply to us."

"Yeah." She took my hand from her head and put it around her waist. "Some would."

In the morning, or what would be the afternoon to most, Eleni said, "I'm so curious. I have to know." She was looking down at me with her black eyes. "How do you actually get the pot when you're done? Do you shit in a Ziploc bag and send it to the guy like that?"

"Yeah, via bike messenger."

"No, really. I know, you think I'm crazy, but I'm just curious. How you gonna do it? You just pick the pellets out of your shit? Do you poke around with a stick, or what?"

"You just . . . you know . . . like, shit in a colander."

"A *colander?*"

"Then rinse it off."

"A fucking colander!"

"You got a better idea?"

"Yeah. Don't go. Try to be sane about one thing in your life."

"You think I'm insane about everything?"

"About some things."

"Like what?"

"Guess."

"I had a feeling this was going here. I'm just trying to figure it out. And I don't know why I'm catching so much shit for that."

"You're not catching any shit from me. You do what you gotta do. Look, I know, you're young, you still have a few good years of pussy-hound left in you, why waste them, right?"

"Eleni, we're not even having sex."

"Yes, and why?"

"Because . . ."

"Forget it. You know what, why don't you go off and do your own thing."

"Do my own thing? What's that mean?"

"You know what it means. Then if you're ever ready to be here, you let me know."

"I'm just— Shit. I'm just trying to make myself happy."

"So am I. But this is making me insane."

"I don't want you to feel insane."

"Yes, I know, you just want me to be happy, too, you've said that already. But I'm not happy this way, does that make sense?"

"Maybe happiness and sanity are an impossible combination. You ever think of that?"

"No."

"Can't we talk about this when I get back?"

"We just finished talking. I am especially finished talking."

"Can't I call you when I get back and—"

"To let me know you're not in a Jamaican prison, you can call me."

"I will."

"And that's it."

THE FLIGHT TO Jamaica was smooth and the hotel wasn't bad for a drug runner's budget. Beyond the street, which ran in front of the hotel, was the beach. On the street there was a taxi driver standing outside his cab. He was very tall, very dark-skinned and had long dreadlocks. He felt shady and he put me on guard. I didn't want to look at him, but my head just clicked in his direction and we made eye contact. He just belted out his pitch. "Yes, Flowers is here for you. You need a ride?"

I said, "No, thanks."

"Where you going?"

"I'm just going down to the beach. I don't need a ride."

"How long will you be in Jamaica?"

"Only for a little while."

"Tell me, what are you going to do?"

"I just want to hang out on the beach, thanks."

"You want to see Jamaica? I will show you Jamaica. Flowers can show you beautiful Jamaica. Why you just want to see your hotel?"

"It's a nice hotel."

"But why you want to eat only your meals here and spend everyday here? Ocho Rios is beautiful. I can show you."

I had flashbacks to guys in Times Square who used to try and get me to walk into an alley with them.

"I'm OK, man."

As I crossed the street he said, "OK, you all right. Yeah, you all right."

I didn't quite know what was up with the guy. I wasn't totally convinced he had sleazy motives. There was also something amiable about him. Yeah, he was being pushy about the ride he wanted to take me on. He genuinely seemed to be disappointed that I didn't want him to take me around so he could show me what he loved about Ocho Rios. It could've been my heightened trepidation that led me to believe every guy in Jamaica was somehow tied in to drug deals with Americans. Two out of the next three days I saw that same guy waiting outside the hotel looking for a fare. And asking me if I wanted to see his beautiful Jamaica.

Twelve o'clock Thursday I was to meet Andre at an outdoor bar on the beach. I was to give him the money and then the next night he would deliver me the marijuana.

I walked out of the hotel, money in my bag, now actually needing a taxi.

"Yes, my friend. Flowers is here."

"I need a ride Mr. Flowers."

"What is your name?"

"Joe."

"I give you a ride wherever you want to go, Joseph, but you don't have to call me Mister. Everyone calls me Flowers."

"OK."

"Where do you go?"

"I have to go to this bar on the ocean next to the Princess Hotel. Do you know it?"

"Oh, yes," he said. "Of course you do."

I didn't know what he meant by that. I thought it better to not ask.

On the ride to the bar there was a flash shower.

"Liquid sunshine," Flowers said. He was so happy about the rain. "We got some liquid sunshine." Then he looked back at me. "You don't have to worry, Joseph. The sun always come back out."

"I'm not worried."

Not really.

When we pulled up to the bar, I knew what Flowers meant by "Of course you do." It was like walking into Spring Break at Daytona Beach. College kids were playing volleyball and doing shots off each other's necks. I thought, OK, smart for Andre and Gil to pick a place where I don't stick out too much.

"Here it is," Flowers said. "Your home away from home."

I paid him, gave him a nice tip and he said, "I told you the sun would be out again." Then, with that genuine disappointment again, he said, "You have yourself a good time now."

"OK, thanks for the ride, Flowers."

"Goodbye, my friend."

I sat down at the bar and ordered a beer. One of the bartenders, an extremely gorgeous local girl who seemed to be in her mid-twenties, was wearing denim shorts cut above the crease of her ass and a tight bikini top. She was flipping beers and catching them behind her and throwing liquor bottles upside down. And every time she reached inside the beer cooler, she'd grind up against the corner of it to the rhythm of the music, her hands pulling out the bottle in slow motion. She had a great act. I guess I was staring, because one of the other bartenders, a guy, came up to me and said, "You like her?"

Trying to play it safe I said, "She's a good bartender."

He laughed at my attempt to play innocent. "You know she will do anything for you."

I just smiled at him.

"I mean, for real. It's no problem. Anything you want."

"Not for me, thanks."

"Then whatchu looking for?"

He had a point. What was I doing there all by myself, not playing volleyball or licking tequila off someone's neck like all the other kids? But I stared at him and played confused.

"You looking for Andre?"

Then, realizing I was that obvious, I said, "You know Andre?"

"Ya, mon. Look over here."

He pointed to four Jamaican guys at a table on the other side of the bar.

"Go 'head," the bartender said. "There is what you are looking for."

I approached the table and two of the guys looked especially alarmed. I said, "I'm looking for Andre."

"Who is looking for Andre?"

"I am."

"And who are you?"

"Are you Andre?" I said.

"No, I ain't Andre."

"I guess I got the wrong guy." Something in me said to get the fuck out of there. Anyone who knows an American punk is looking for Andre probably knows that same American punk is also carrying a nice wad of money.

He said, "What's your name?"

"Never mind." I started to walk away.

"Whatchu looking for? We got what you want."

"I only talk to Andre. I gotta go."

"You can talk to me. Whatchu need?"

I put a stop-sign hand out in front of me and backpedaled. "Nothing. I don't need anything. It's no problem."

I walked back to where the taxis were and Flowers was still there waiting for a fare. "Hello, my friend. You finished already?"

"Yeah, I want to go back to the hotel." My voice was shaky.

"I take you, Joseph."

We rode in silence for a few blocks.

"What happened, Joseph? You didn't see no American girls you liked?"

I actually loved listening to this guy speak. He had a sweet Jamaican accent peppered with "hey's" and "mon's." His voice actually calmed me down.

"Yeah," I said. "I guess I was being shy."

"Oh, you ain't shy. I can see you. You see these kids when they come here from United States, from Canada, I don't mean you, but Jamaica brings out the worst in them, and that is not what Jamaica is. So I want to show you something different, my friend." He looked at me in the rearview mirror. "I can see you. I know you want to see what else we have."

"What do you want to show me?"

"This is a beautiful place. We're happy just because we have the day. I can show you beautiful Jamaica."

"OK, Flowers, show me."

"Ya, mon?"

"Yeah, man. Show me."

"Yes, Joseph! I will show you! I will show you!"

We drove for a while through the hills and Flowers was right, it became gorgeous. Everything was overgrown and wild and it was so much more beautiful than it was near the bay, where the hotels were. Nobody licking tequila off anyone's neck up here. Then I started to see a few houses. Outside one house, which was really a shack, there were four girls playing double-dutch jump rope who looked like they could have been on an Olympic team. One girl was jumping through the ropes with another, smaller girl on her back. I said to Flowers, "Why do they call you Flowers?"

"Because I am sooooo pretty, mon."

Flowers stopped the cab on the side of the road and said, "Come with me, Joseph."

Yes. Bag full of money on me, twenty minutes after the locals had just tried to take me, in the middle of the hills, with no one around—yes. I went with him. I just felt like I could.

We walked a trail through the trees and it opened up to the top of a waterfall. Ya, mon—an actual tropical fucking waterfall, like you read about. About forty feet below us there were a group of kids. Eight of them, from maybe six to nine years old, playing in the water. Flowers yelled, "Haile! Daddy is here." Then we walked down the side of the waterfall toward the kids.

With a huge smile on his face, Flowers said, "Haile, say hello to Joseph." And he did. These kids had no trouble adjusting to the new American guy. Within two minutes they were taking turns jumping off my shoulders into the actual tropical fucking waterfall, yelling, "Joseph, Joseph, me next!" and they had me trying to catch frogs with them on the riverbank.

After a while, Flowers tied his wet dreadlocks up behind his head and told Haile it was time to eat dinner. "Joseph," Flowers said. "You will come eat with us, yes?"

"Yeah, I'll come with you." I didn't realize I was hungry until he mentioned food. I'd forgotten I hadn't had lunch. I'd forgotten about the time. I'd forgotten about the scary run-in at the bar, I'd even forgotten about all the money that was in my bag. I'd forgotten why I was in Jamaica in the first place.

Haile carried a frog with him all the way up the hill to his father's taxi and held it for the whole ride home. We pulled up to the shack where they lived. It was surrounded by trees and huge green plants that were unfamiliar to me. A clothesline stretched from one side of the house and on the other side was a water pump. Through the trees, not too far off, I could see other houses and could hear tiny voices coming from their direction. Flowers told Haile to let the frog go before he went into the house. Haile protested and Flowers said, "You let him go, he will come back if he wants." Haile put the frog on the ground and it jumped away.

Flowers' wife was named Rosaire. They squeezed hands the way many other couples kiss each other's cheek. Rosaire wasn't all smiles the way Flowers was. She seemed to be put off by the stranger her husband had just brought home and she shot me a hard, skeptical look. Then she welcomed me. "Joseph from America," she said. "Hello."

We sat at a table outside and before we ate they said a prayer in a language I didn't understand. She served us bread and stew. I couldn't tell you exactly what was in the stew. Some kind of meat with an unfamiliar texture, but it was great. Haile kept looking to the trees to see, I imagined, if his frog would come back.

When we finished, Haile asked Flowers to push him on a rope that was tied to a high tree branch. They ran off behind the house. Rosaire said, "So, Joseph from America, you like our country?"

"I do. I'm glad I got to see more of it. Thanks to Flowers."

"Yes, my husband is very friendly. He is very trusting." Then she leaned closer to me and lowered her voice. "Maybe I am not."

Instantly I felt I was sitting in front of a fortune-teller who had some bad news about me.

"You came by yourself," she said.

"Yes."

"Your lady didn't want to come with you?"

"No."

This woman was on to me from minute one.

"Why not?"

I couldn't answer.

"It's not my business why you came to Jamaica, that is true. But you are in our home now. Yes?"

I nodded.

"So whatever you take back with you does not involve us. Yes?"

"Right."

"You know if something is good or not, right, Joseph?"

"Yes, I do."

Can every woman with dark eyes see through me?

"Good. Because your friend Flowers, he trusts you."

"I understand."

Rosaire took the dishes to the water pump.

Flowers came from behind the house. "Joseph, I want to show you something."

Inside their shack, two blankets were hung as a partition and Flowers took me into the makeshift room. There was a mattress on the floor with clean-looking blankets, and in the corner there was what looked like a shrine. Three candles in front of two pictures: one of Jesus and one of someone I didn't recognize.

"I know who that is," I said. "But who's that?"

"He was the Emperor of Ethiopia. Haile Selassie."

"You named your son after an emperor, huh?"

"Yes. I don't know if he was a great man. I know he wanted to be. Even great men are flawed. Let me show you something." He reached behind the picture of Jesus and pulled out an American one-hundred-dollar bill. "This is a gift from my friend. He was here three years ago. This was his gift to me and my family."

"That was generous of him," I said.

"We offer it to them and pray that more will come back." Then Flowers let out a smile that lived up to his name. I wanted to reach in my bag, pull out another hundred and say, "Here, Flowers. Your prayers have not been in vain." But I couldn't. All I had was drug money. And Rosaire knew it. It would have been an insult. So I said nothing. I looked, with Flowers, into the eyes of an emperor and remained incapable of gift-giving.

"I have to work again, Joseph. Come, I'll drive you back to the bay."

It was the first thing I saw when I walked out of their shack. At first it looked like a rock. Just a gray lump on the ground. Then I noticed it was looking right at me. It was Haile's frog. The sun had started to set and dropped a light mustard on the left side of its body. For a second this tiny thing charmed me into stillness. I was completely stiff, upright and slightly swaying like a cobra.

"Haile, your friend is here."

Haile came from the side of the shack, walked carefully to the frog and picked it up. The frog didn't even jump. When I said goodbye, Rosaire stood with Haile tucked between her stomach and her arm.

When we got back to the hotel, I said, "What do I owe you, Flowers?"

"You don't owe me anything."

"I mean, how much was the ride?"

He only charged me the amount of money it cost to get from the bar to my hotel.

Then I got on the phone to New York.

"Hello?"

"Gil, it's Joseph—it's Joe.

"What happened?"

"I couldn't find Andre at the bar today."

"Yeah, I know. Andre will meet you outside your hotel tomorrow night at ten o'clock. OK?"

"I'll be there."

"Good."

Then he hung up.

THE NEXT NIGHT, at ten o'clock, there were three guys waiting for me outside the hotel. Two of them had machetes in their belts. I walked over and looked at the one guy who wasn't displaying a weapon. He said, "You are Joe?"

"Yeah."

"I'm Andre. Come with us."

I got into the car and took the longest fifteen-minute ride of my life. We went way into the mountains on a road scattered with occasional shacks far from any tourist activity or light. They stopped the car in front of one of the shacks and told me to step inside. There was a time delay between when my mind told my legs to move and when they actually moved. Andre closed the door, stood in front of me and the two thugs stood behind me.

"Where's the money?"

How quickly I went from having a beer with a guy in a Hell's Kitchen bar to a shack in Jamaica surrounded by three guys with machetes who wanted to know where their money was.

I said, "I have it," not sure if this was the right time to take it out.

"I always get the money before you get your stuff."

"I looked for you at the bar yesterday to give it to you then. That's what Gil Z said to do."

He was unimpressed.

"Give it to me now."

When he finished counting it, Andre nodded to one of the thugs. The guy left the shack, then returned with a yellow plastic bag filled with compressed marijuana pellets. Tomorrow's breakfast.

I put it in my knapsack and said, "Are we OK?"

"Yes, we are OK. Let's go."

When we pulled up to my hotel, I saw Flowers outside, looking for a fare. I spotted him before he saw me and I had a quick, guilty impulse to hide before he caught me stepping out of Andre's car. But he turned and saw me before I could bolt. He smiled. Then paused. Took in the scene. Kept the smile on his lips but let it leave his eyes.

I walked over to him.

"Hi, Flowers."

"Joseph, what are you doing?"

"I just wanted to say thank you again for last night. I think you're all great people. You and your family. I had a great time."

He repeated, "What are you doing, my friend?"

I couldn't answer him. I'd just gotten out of a drug dealer's car at eleven o'clock at night. What was there to say?

"Listen, I'm going to need a ride to the airport tomorrow afternoon."

"Yes?"

"So . . ." I waited, like an idiot, for him to offer.

"Well, I had a great time yesterday. So thanks again. OK?"

"It was nothing," he said. Then he turned to a well-dressed couple who'd just stepped out of the hotel and said, "Yes, Flowers is here!"

SWALLOWING LATEX-COVERED marijuana pellets is unpleasant.

They were cylinders about one inch long and one-half inch in diameter. Some were bigger. When I tried to swallow the first one, it felt as if someone wearing surgical gloves were checking my gag reflex. It went halfway down my throat, then came back up. I coughed, I breathed, attempted to relax my throat and tried again.

Same results.

It had never occurred to me that I wouldn't be able to swallow them. Not until that moment. I knew if I didn't do it, if I came home with nothing, I was into Gil Z for the cost of the vacation and the pot. I knew two other things: One, I didn't have that kind of money; and two, Gil Z had the gun.

With a glass of water I tried to take the pellet down like a vitamin. I swallowed the water, but the pellet got stuck. It took two more sips of water to finally get the pellet down my throat. Great. One down, ninety-nine left.

Even with the water I was still gagging some of them back up. And some of the bigger ones took three or four tries. I was nauseous with latex and water. I thought, am I gonna throw them up and have to do it all over again? The words *fucking nightmare* crossed my mind. In the mirror, I said, "How do you feel now, cowboy?"

It took almost three hours and two gallons of water. Then it was time to check out and get to the airport. I walked to the lobby still on the verge of throwing up but laughed when the woman at the front desk asked me if I enjoyed my stay.

Outside the hotel there were plenty of cabs but no Flowers. The new cabdriver had nothing to say. He was busy listening to two guys on a political radio station talk about what a powerful country the United States is.

AS SOON AS the plane took off I started reading a book, and about twenty minutes into it I realized I was still on the same paragraph. I had read it sixty times and had no idea what it said. When I lifted my head from the book, I had this feeling in the back of my neck as if a bunch of hot rubber bands had contracted to raise my skull.

I was stoned outta my friggin' bird.

I hadn't smoked pot in over four years. It made me tired, hungry, stupid and, worst of all, paranoid. The only thoughts I could sustain were of me getting arrested when I got to New York. How the fuck am I gonna get through customs in this condition? I can't smell like pot. Or can I? No, I never burned anything. My breath was latex and my eyes were probably neon signs advertising my state. I gotta take a look at myself. I got up from my seat. Am I standing? Yes, I'm standing. As I walked toward the bathroom, the chairs on each side of the aisle ahead of me, in the rhythm of my heartbeat, started moving closer together, making my passage smaller and smaller.

I made it to the bathroom door, but I couldn't figure out how to open it. After pulling on the wrong handle, leaning all my weight into it and coming just short of kicking it, a stewardess came over and simply pulled the correct latch and the door swung open, almost by itself. I said, "Oh, thank you." I smiled at her and said, "Must be jet lag." Which made a lot of fucking sense. What I should have said was, *See? This is why I stopped smoking pot four years ago.*

In the mirror, thankfully, my eyes weren't red. OK, cool. But more importantly, what are mirrors made of? Not the glass part, but the part that reflects? What is that stuff? Joey, you have to calm the fuck down. There is really no way for anyone to tell that you're high. They'll just think you're stupid. And you'd have to agree with them.

Five hours. In this condition, on an airplane, for five . . . hours. And when that's over? Customs. I couldn't even figure out how to open the bathroom fuckin' door. Perfect time to be under a drug-induced paranoia. Perfect. I didn't understand. The pellets were wrapped in latex, I thought, you can't digest latex. But you can digest pot. One of the pellets must have snapped open. Then I had the most terrifying thought of all: *How many of them snapped open?*

And how many of them are *going* to snap open?

I made it back to my seat, on my first try, and I looked out the window. Being above the clouds was beautiful. To look out at the atmosphere and know I was traveling four hundred miles an hour at thirty-five thousand feet wasn't scary at all. Everything was so still and peaceful out there; much better conditions out there than in my own body.

So I'll just look out the window for as long as I can and deal with the hell that is my own mind. I won't try to come up with good defense for communism; I'll bury my face in this book, pray no one talks to me and try to ignore the chicken or steak that they'll serve for dinner.

Four and a half hours and two pages later, the captain

announced that we were about to land in New York on a clear
Saturday night. It was sixty-nine degrees at 9:34 P.M. From that
height, all I could make out of the city were its lights. New York
looked like it had a white sun living underneath it and someone
had punched thousands of tiny holes in the ground. I got out of
my seat, grabbed my duffel bag from the overhead compartment
and began to slowly file out with all the other passengers.

First corridor, fifteen police officers and five police dogs. The
cops holding the dogs wore plain clothes and had their badges
hanging from a chain on their necks. They seemed to have more
authority. When I caught sight of their badges, I realized why:
They were Drug Enforcement agents. One of the dogs poked his
nose at my knee. I looked down at him and let out a sound like
"Oooh," as if to say, *look how cute,* and went to pet him. It seemed
to be the kind of thing a sober person who wasn't afraid of police
dogs trained to detect marijuana from two miles away would do.
The cop pulled on his leash and in his best Irish-Drug-
Enforcement-agent-from-Queens accent yelled, "Don't touch
duh dogs, people! Don't touch duh dogs!" I kept moving.

There was a guy and his girlfriend who looked like they'd just
gotten out of a Judas Priest concert and the cop yelled, "Hey, we
got Metallica here tonight. Check it out!" The guy did look to
see which cop was yelling, but knew better than to say anything.
I developed an instant love affair with this kid and his girlfriend
and tried to walk as close to them as possible. They made me
look like I'd just spent a weekend at a shuffleboard tournament
in Boca Raton and was on my way back to Greenwhich.

Finally the corridor led to customs. Arriving passengers had to
wait in a roped-off waiting line about thirty people long. At the
front of the line a woman was directing people to one of twelve
six-foot inspection tables. Each table was manned by two customs
officers. One to look at your luggage, one to look at you. While I
was waiting on line I saw a scraggly kid about my age who had the
entire contents of his suitcase emptied out on the table. The customs officer was going through his socks. The only part of the

conversation I could hear was the kid trying to convince the officer that he had been sober for three years. I thought, I hear you kid, almost four years for me. If you don't count the past six hours.

When I reached the front of the line, the woman directed me to table number five. When I walked to table five, there were four officers there who didn't look as if they were inspecting bags. One of them was sitting on the table. That didn't seem right. I said, "Excuse me? Can I come through here?"

The guy who liked his job the least answered me. "Did someone tell you you could come through here?"

"That woman over there told me to come to table five."

"I don't think she did, because you can't come through here. Go back and ask her where she wants you to go."

Shit, I thought, I'm too stoned and stupid to even walk to the right table. I got back to the woman and said, "Excuse me? They told me I couldn't go to table five?"

She looked back at table five, then said, "Oh, I'm sorry." And, without realizing how close she'd come to inspiring cardiac arrest in a complete stranger, said, "Go to table eleven."

"Thank you." And thank Christ that wasn't my fault.

When I got to table eleven, I said "Hi!" and the officer said:

"Open the bag, please."

"Sure!"

He manhandled his way through it.

"Where you coming from?"

"Jamaica."

"How long were you there?"

"Five days."

"Where'd you stay?"

"Ocho Rios."

"Where do you live?"

"Manhattan."

"What neighborhood?"

"Hell's Kitchen. Although it's not so hellish anymore." I figured a little light conversation couldn't hurt.

"Yeah, that's right."

He was quiet for a moment, then produced a small case wrapped in a rubber band.

"Open this for me."

"Sure."

He was staring directly at my hands, I was guessing, to see if they were shaking or not. I got the rubber band off without incident and showed him the bar of soap that was in the case.

"Take the soap out of the case."

"Sure."

As I did, he said, "Where'd you stay in Jamaica?"

Fuck. Why was he was trying to catch me in a lie? I said, "Ocho Rios?"

"Oh. Nice there?"

"Yeah, it's really nice."

Then he leaned over the table and locked eyes with me like a well-trained screen actor during his close-up and said, "What'd you do there?"

My heart dropped out of my ass.

"Mostly worked on a screenplay with my cowriter. Happy to get out of the city for a while."

No idea where that came from.

"You write screenplays?"

"Yeah." I let out a little laugh. "I'm trying. Selling it's the hard part, though," as I stood there with a bar of soap in one hand and a pound of contraband in my stomach. Or intestines. Or colon. Or bloodstream. Or wherever the fuck it was at that point.

"Yeah, sure," he said. "You can pack your stuff up."

I said, "OK." I put everything back in my bag, said "Thank you," and walked the fuck out of there as calmly as I possibly could with my newfound phobia of soap cases and customs officers.

THE SHUTTLE BUS from the airport let me off at Grand Central. I went to a pay phone to call Eleni and got her answering machine.

"Eleni it's me. Are you there? Hello? Hello, hello? All right, well, I made it home OK. I'm at Grand Central was just gonna start walking, I guess—"

She picked up the phone. "Hello."

"Oh, you're there."

"Are you OK?"

"Yeah, I got a story for you, this is unreal—"

"You should probably take a cab home instead of walking. Don't you think?"

"Um, yeah. Well, I was thinking—I just want to tell you about the trip. I thought I would come over there, if that's, you know, if that's OK."

"I don't think so, Joe."

There was a silence.

Then she said, "It's not a good idea. I just wanted to make sure you got in OK. That's all."

"Yeah, all right, that's OK. Maybe I'll call you tomorrow. I'll talk to you then."

" 'Bye," she said.

"OK. 'Bye."

What I didn't say was that I *definitely* wanted to call her tomorrow—first thing in the morning. I was afraid to say that. But if I was so afraid, then why didn't I? That would've been riding out into a frontier. And maybe, in some way, scarier than going to jail.

I WALKED WEST on 42nd Street toward Hell's Kitchen. In Times Square, the Broadway shows were just getting out and the streets were packed.

Then I noticed him walking toward me. He looked homeless, but wasn't carrying anything with him. The left side of his face was twitching. He wiped his nose with his sleeve and was sniffing like a dog. It felt like a disease was walking at me. I thought, *This guy's fucking nuts.* Two steps away from me, he suddenly looked as if he were about to do something that would bring him perverse pleasure. As he passed me, and with a calm, directed anger, he whispered "You think I'm fucking nuts." What the fuck was that? I know I'm friggin' blitzed right now but did that guy just rip a thought right out of my head?

I couldn't move.

Two small crowds of people came from both directions and snapped me out of it. They bumped into me, trying to get past me on the sidewalk. Attempting to get out of their way, I crashed into a couple of them. I said, "I'm sorry, I'm sorry." I went chest to chest with some guy and we did that thing two people do when they are trying to get out of each other's way, and we both made a move in the same direction. We went back and forth three times, then finally he said, "Why don't you just stand still, man." I did and he walked around me. It seemed like the perfect time to sit the fuck down. I landed on the sidewalk, with my back against a building.

I reflected on the busy day's activities. Woke up in Jamaica, swallowed a pound of marijuana, almost had a heart attack in customs, tried to make friends with a police goddamn dog, some guy who I thought was out of his mind just whispered my own thoughts back to me and now I'm sitting on the sidewalk in Times Square. This is what I asked for. The hero's journey thing. The menacing museum after closing time. The how-much-cowboy-can-this-cowboy-take? adventure. It was a Saturday night on the streets of New York—the land of misfit subjects who, by permission of their Creator, jump off their canvas, out of their frame, break their sculpted positions and all mingle to try and make sense of one another. This entourage of strange and bizarre creatures had two things to say to me: *"We'll take your mind and we'll make you stand still."*

I went to another pay phone.

"Hey, it's me again. Could you pick up? Just for a second? I want you to hear this, because there's stuff going on here. Hello? I just want to tell you that I think we should stand still. I want to find out what'll happen if we stood still in front of each other.

Because people are telling me that that's the thing to do. And I believe it. They're talking to me, these creatures—I mean these people. If you stand still in front of your fears, something else can happen. You know? Is this making any sense? Eleni, could you please pick up and just tell me if this makes sense to you? Hello? Eleni? Eleni? All right, maybe I'm just a little out of it right now. I know I might sound crazy but . . . I'll try to explain it some other time, then. All right, I'll just . . . OK. OK. 'Bye."

With no one left to call, I started pleading with all these people around me. *OK then,* I was saying, *take my mind and make me still.* Nobody whispered any assurances back to me. I kept asking. *Take my mind and make me still.* Except I knew I couldn't do it that night. It was too loud. I jumped at every sound and my head was going at breakneck speed. I wanted to be still—like the clouds at thirty-five thousand feet. Or like a waterfall. Like a Jamaican frog. But I couldn't. I felt so horribly alive. I couldn't be still and give up my mind right then. No chance. Not tonight. And not even the next day. Because all I could do the next day was wake up and sell the drugs that were in my body.

remember the barbecues most. I was nine, ten, eleven, or so, and I can see them clearly. That night on the street, however, stands out more like a dream. I sometimes have to remind myself that it was actual, not an imagined thing. Maybe it's because I don't understand it as well as I think I do. If so, that'll remain as is. I mean, I can't bring myself to ask her about it.

GINGY

The barbecues happened at my Aunt Connie and Uncle Gingy's house, on Nepperhan Avenue in southwest Yonkers, and they were huge. Forty or fifty people would show up. Embroidered tablecloths were put over picnic tables, and a canopy of string lights, with bulbs the shape of red peppers, were hung over the back porch. Kids played Wiffle ball on the side of the house, and the old men sat at a card table where they cursed in the mother tongue. My aunt and uncle turned their yard into an all-you-can-eat Italian feast. This was my father's side of the family—the Frascones. Gingy was my dad's younger brother.

Uncle Gingy is the kind of guy who—as they say—should not

be fucked with. There were many legends that floated around the family that supported that warning. There was the incident with the used car salesman. This was before he did time. Gingy bought this car and as it turned out there were more things wrong with it than the guy had explained. Gingy took the car back a few days later and told the guy he wanted his three thousand dollars back. The salesman said that was impossible. Gingy asked the salesman to come outside—there was something he needed to see. Gingy took the tire iron out of his car and smashed the windshield of another car and told the salesman that if he didn't get his money back he was going to do more than three thousand dollars' worth of damage. He said, "If you call the cops, they'll get me for destruction of private property. I'll have to go to court, it'll take three months for my case to come up, then they'll make me pay for all this. When that's all over, I'll come for you."

Five minutes and two more windshields later, they were in the office, the salesman counting out three thousand dollars in Franklins. This is how business is done in Yonkers.

Telling stories was a contact sport for Uncle Gingy and listening to him was one of my favorite parts of the barbecues. They fascinated my ten-year-old mind but were tough on the body. For emphasis, he would grab me by the back of my neck or give me an open-hand slap on the spine with enough force to put out a skinny dog. But there was no way I was letting on how much it hurt to listen. I would laugh and flinch while still trying to stay attentive.

"So, I did a job on Mclean Avenue, Joey. The Side Car Saloon. It's a bar. The guy's ceiling had been falling for two decades. The way I see it, he had twenty grand worth of fines for violating codes, no doubt. Fire inspectors didn't even write him up. Big fuckin' surprise there. You can't grease the fire inspectors, you can't grease a thirty-dollar whore."

My father chimed in while he was walking by, "Gingy, you wanna watch your mouth in fronna my kid."

"What? He knows. The kid's not dumb." Uncle Gingy put me in the first headlock of the story. "Joey, what your father doesn't tell you, I will. So, long story short, we fix the guy's ceiling and he mails me payment with a letter: Dear mister whatever, this is the first installment, bullshit, blah, blah, bullshit . . . The check was one-tenth of what the job was. How many installments did he plan on, right? So I go over there. I say to the guy, 'Look, what fuckin' installments? Gimme the rest and give it to me in cash.' Why should I trust this guy's checks at this point? Guy's like, 'No, no, no, hold on a second, my business is off thirty percent, we can work something out.' Bullshit, right? I told 'em, I said, 'Look, you gotta ante up. I don't care your business is off, my guys gotta eat, too. You got enough to grease the fire department, but you can't pay me for the job?' I said, 'You don't want me to make a scene they'll hear in Dublin.' He's goin', 'I'll give you another installment by next month.' I said, 'Next month? You wanna make a deal? Here's the deal,' I told him."

Uncle Gingy called out to his wife. "Connie."

"What, Gingy?"

"Make me another sandwich?"

She picked up a plate.

" 'So here's the deal,' I told him. I go behind the bar. He's got an old-time cash register with push buttons, right? The numbers pop up in the back when it rings. I lift the fuckin' thing right from behind the bar. I said, 'The deal is, I get this and whatever's in it and you get it back empty when you come clean.' "

Gingy started laughing. I braced myself and got the open-hand slap to the back. "Joey, this friggin' thing was so goddamn heavy I thought I was gonna die. But I can't stop there, right? I do that, I look like a jerk. It woulda ruined my whole show, right? So, I get to the door, I can't open it. I'm kickin' it, pushin' up against it. I'm not lettin' the fuckin' cash register go. The fuckin' guy comes over and opens the fuckin' door. Holds it open so I can walk out. I can't even hold back the laughs. This moron clown was so scared he helped me steal his own cash register. Fuckin' riot, right? I didn't know whether to shit, whistle or go blind. And, let me tell you, he paid up. OK?"

Then he got me in another headlock and right into my ear said, "Sometimes, Joey, all bets are off and you gotta make your own rules. You know what I mean?"

"Yeah," I said.

"You gotta be smart, but you gotta know what kinda smart you are. Do me a favor, get your Uncle Gingy another beer, will ya?"

"Sure."

I started to go.

"Wait a minute," he said. "Come over here. This is bothering me." He was looking at my clothes with disgust. "Your father dress you like that? With your collar tucked in your sweater? You look as gay as Christmas tinsel." He grabbed my collar between his thumb and forefinger, with his pinkie extended like he was raising a shot glass, lifted it out of my sweater, and smoothed it down. "Always look smart, Joey." He gave me another headlock, kissed me on the head, then whacked me on my ass so hard it stung like a bee colony. "You gotta be careful what you wear these days. The fashion industry's not gonna stop until they turn us all into faggots."

I went over to the cooler to get him another beer. My aunt was at the table next to me making Gingy's sandwich. She lifted some cold cuts from the platter and then she called to him to ask if he wanted mustard or mayonnaise. His response was, "Twenty years and she still wants to know if I want mustard or mayonnaise. Jesus." Connie calmly spread mustard on the bread. She shook her head and, so only I could hear, said, "Ah, Joey. Why do I always think he's gonna want something different?"

THE COUSINS

Maria was the youngest, then there were Anthony and Little Gingy—Maria's bodyguards. Cousin Gingy was called Little Gingy only to distinguish him from his father. Little Gingy was not actually little. We also called him Crazy Gingy. Anthony, we called Fat Tony. He actually was fat.

In high school, Maria dated this guy Phillip Gallagher, a kid up the street I used to play kickball with, whom she caught cheating on her. When Maria took Phillip back, Crazy Gingy said, "Maria, I'll tell you one thing about guys who cheat. If you let 'em get away with it once, they'll do it again." Gingy was right, Phillip did it again. So, for fucking over his sister twice, Crazy Gingy broke Phillip's elbow on the outside doorjamb of DiFabio's Pizza, two blocks from Phillip's house. Little Gingy argued that he was merely giving Phillip a piece of advice. "Now he'll be more careful about what he puts his arm around."

At the barbecues, when I wasn't eating or playing Wiffle ball with my cousins, I was with Aunt Connie. She let me sit on the kitchen counter when she was getting the food ready. I was in charge of taste-testing and rubbing cloves of garlic on the insides of the bowls that needed seasoning. She was so pretty to look at.

The longest night I got to spend with her was the night our grandmother died.

My father, his wife and Uncle Gingy went to the hospital. They figured the kids were too young and they could only fit so many people in a hospital room anyway, so my sister, our three cousins and I stayed at Aunt Connie's house.

Connie made us dinner and we all helped. My job was to make the salad. "Aunt Connie, should I rub garlic on the salad bowl?"

"Yeah, why not? It's Saturday night, right?"

After dinner, all five kids fell asleep in the living room with the TV on. I was on the couch with Aunt Connie, my head in her lap. We woke up to the sound of the adults coming home from the hospital. We could sense the news wasn't good. It was my stepmother who told us that our grandmother died. Neither Uncle Gingy nor my father looked any of us kids in the eye. They only started joking around about how skinny we were and how Aunt Connie should have kept us well fed while they were gone; we were growing, after all.

Connie didn't play it that way. She didn't think it was a good time for cracking jokes. She gave every one of us a hug and told us that our grandmother loved us and that she was a good lady. The rest of the adults went to the kitchen to eat. Crazy Gingy and Fat Tony went up to their rooms. Maria stayed on the couch with my sister and me. My head wound up back in my aunt's lap. I remember her playing with my hair until I fell asleep again.

BLINDFOLDED

At one barbecue, the adults played the blindfold game. This was the same day I heard my father and stepmother talking in the car.

One person would sit in a chair with a blindfold on. All the members of the opposite sex came up to that person one by one. By feeling only one body part the blindfolded person had to identify their husband or wife.

When it was Uncle Gingy's turn, all he could touch was the left side of the women's faces. He put his hand on the first three women and instantly said "No" each time. Then Aunt Connie walked up to him. He put one hand on her cheek and said nothing. He raised his other hand to her other cheek, pulled her face to his mouth and kissed her lips then, pulled her down to his lap, said "This is my girl," and gave her a huge hug—still blindfolded.

Then they put the blindfold on Gingy's Cousin Jimmy. He was allowed to touch the women's upper arms. When my Aunt Connie approached him, his hand wandered up her sleeve all the way to her neck. "Yeah, this is mine," he said. Then he took off the blindfold and saw it was Connie. He kept his hand up her shirt while he apologized to his wife. Everyone was laughing except Uncle Gingy.

Later in the day, after Uncle Gingy had a few in him, he said to Jimmy, "One thing you don't mess with is family, Jimmy."

"What are you talkin' about?"

"You know what I'm talkin' about. You think just because you had the blindfold on it means you didn't know what you were touching?"

"Gingy, get over it, all right. It's just a game."

"Get over it? What I should get over is the fact that you use the game as an excuse to act like an asshole."

"Only one of us is acting like an asshole."

Gingy threw his beer across the lawn; it smashed against the back fence and silenced everyone. My father jumped between Gingy and Jimmy. "That's enough," my father said. "You're acting like a bunch of babies."

"Who's an asshole, Jimmy?"

My father said, "Cut it out. There's kids over here."

I was next to Aunt Connie, her hand on my shoulder. Crazy Gingy, at eight years old, was trying to figure out which guy to stand up to. My sister and Cousin Maria were tearing up.

Then my father lowered his voice a little. "You want everyone to know what goes on when your doors are closed? You're makin' a jerk outta yourself."

By then two other cousins had stepped between Gingy and Jimmy.

Jimmy said, "All right, I'm leaving, Gingy. You happy? Nice fuckin' barbecue. You're a real gentleman."

Uncle Gingy said, "And you, Jimmy, you're a speck a' cum."

"That's enough!" Now my father was in Gingy's face. "In fronna your daughter you talk like that?"

Gingy turned to see his daughter Maria, holding on to her neck with both hands.

Gingy said, "Don't worry, Maria, Cousin Jimmy's goin' home now." He turned to Jimmy. "He'll be gone when I come out of the house." On his way into the house, he walked past Aunt Connie and said, "He keep his hand up your shirt long enough?"

NAPPY NOODLE

The highway lights made shadows float through the car and put my sister to sleep in a minute. I lay there with my eyes closed, getting jiggled by the bumps on the road. The twenty-minute ride from Yonkers to my father's apartment in Port Chester was silent until my stepmother brought it up.

"Your brother was in rare form tonight."

"What else is new?"

"I've never seen him like that before."

"You didn't share a room with him for seventeen years."

"Does he have a history with Jimmy?"

"Are the kids asleep?"

"I think so."

"Hey, guys?" my father said.

No sounds from the back seat.

"It's not what my brother has with Jimmy, it's with Connie."

"What did she do?"

"Nothin'. She never does anything wrong. She's like a breathing saint, that woman."

"So what's his problem?"

"Guy's got a woman who looks like that, he thinks everyone's tryin' to steal her. He's always been insane that way. I saw him throw a beatin' on a guy once for helping Connie carry groceries home from the store."

"What?"

"Yeah, when they first started dating, they were just kids, I'll never forget, Nappy Noodle, this guy from the neighborhood—"

"Wait, what was this guy's name?"

"Nappy Noodle. That wasn't his name, that's just what we called him. Nappy helped Connie carry a bag of groceries home from the store to her mother's house. Gingy got word of it and beat the shit out of Nappy. Hit him on toppa the head with the butt of his gun like he was drivin' a nail."

"Hit him with *what*?" My stepmother sounded incredulous.

"The butt of his gun."

"Oh, my God."

"Nappy went into his shoes. It took three guys—me, Carmine and Ernie—to stop Gingy. We thought he was gonna kill 'im. There was blood on the street. I swear on my eyes, that's how it happened. Gingy gets his knickers twisted over that shit, nobody's safe around him. Especially not Connie. He'll probably beat her up tonight."

"You *serious*?"

"Sure. You kiddin'? After thirty years you think I don't know my brother?"

When Uncle Gingy said "the one thing you don't mess with is family," he failed to mention that his motto applied to wives in complicated ways. I was baffled by the idea that the same hands that blindly picked my Aunt Connie's cheek out of a crowd could so easily turn on her. While I pretended to sleep, new pictures of Uncle Gingy came to me. The Uncle Gingy I hadn't been introduced to until that night. The one ready to cause all the indiscriminate ruin of a land mine in his own house. I could see my cousins tiptoeing around him. If all that my father had said was true, if his prediction of what was going to happen to my aunt was actually happening, then why, I thought, were we driving in the opposite direction?

JONAH

It took the assault of a police officer to put Uncle Gingy away. It was a night of debauchery with his cronies and he wound up outside a bar, about to be cited for disturbing the peace. Gingy challenged the officer to show him where the peace was. He said, "You can't disturb something that doesn't exist."

The cop told him, "There'll be some peace when you shut the fuck up."

"First Amendment tells me I can say whatever I want. And it is my right to know where the peace is that I'm getting cited for disturbing."

The cop put his stick in Gingy's face. "I'll shove your amendment from your throat to your ass. Now, if you don't shut up, you're goin' downtown."

Gingy said, "Let me ask you something . . . fuck you!" and landed a right hook over the cop's left eye. The cop got three stitches, which made it look even worse. If it wasn't for Uncle Gingy's priors he may have gotten away with community service, but it was a felony and the DA treated it like one. He did a year in City and was on probation for another two. After he got out of prison, Uncle Gingy's stories changed drastically.

He took me aside during his welcome-home barbecue.

"It's like this, Joseph. You know the story of Jonah and the whale?"

"He got swallowed by the whale?"

"That's right. You know why?"

"Not really."

"OK. Jonah was this guy. Like every other guy. He was free, walkin' around on earth with everyone else, the sun shining on him just like you and me. Then he was asked to serve God. God asked him to go to the city of Nineveh and spread God's word. Now, Jonah didn't know if he wanted to do that or not. So God took him off the land and put him on a boat. He was closer to being alone then, but still couldn't decide whether or not he wanted to serve God. Then God puts him in the hull of the ship, to row. He's with a lot less people down there, he's got no sun, and still he doesn't know if he wants to serve God. Then the whale comes, wrecks the boat and swallows Jonah. God put Jonah in the whale's mouth. Alone, with no food, no sun, nothin' but himself. And that's what it took for Jonah to decide. That's when Jonah said he would go to the city of Nineveh, spread the word and serve God.

"Joseph, I'm going to tell you the most important thing. Everyone is called by God. Everyone. But not everyone hears the calling. When you hear it—and I know you will—pick the life that serves God. If you're having trouble making up your mind, God will give you the exact circumstances you need to help you decide. He's not going to make the decision for you. No way. Free will is part of the deal when you're human. He didn't tell

Jonah to serve or not to serve; He just helped him decide. And, just like He gave Jonah, He'll give you everything you need to help you make your decision. You may have to be in a dark place, all alone. It might seem scary and impossible, but when God puts you there, believe me, it's a gift."

Then Gingy leaned closer to me. "I think He's already calling you. And if you don't serve Him, Joseph, you'll be stuck in the mouth of a whale for the rest of your life. Alone. In the dark. And you don't want that."

Uncle Gingy was officially scaring me shitless. My family wasn't exactly the God-fearing type. We called ourselves Catholic, but the only time we went to church was when they were giving out props like on Palm Sunday or Ash Wednesday. At worst, mass was vaguely boring, and never terrifying. Although right then, as my uncle looked into me, I was a believer in fear. His eyes were like two dark priests impaling me to a church door for interrogation.

"When I first got to prison, I thought God was just playing with me. I thought he had no good reason for putting me there. It seemed impossible. Now I see. When you hear God calling you to serve Him, all bets are off. He's making the rules. And when it seems like it's never been darker, that's when you'll pick. That's when you'll see there is only one true road."

My father walked over.

"Hey, what are you tellin' my son?"

"The truth."

"Gingy, he's twelve. Give 'im a break."

Uncle Gingy held my father's eyes.

"Joey," my dad said, "Your Aunt Connie just brought out the fried artichokes you like. Go grab some before your uncle has you in a brown robe, swingin' incense."

Uncle Gingy slapped God on me as hard as he would have slapped a fist on someone who, only a year ago, stole money from him. This was a different headlock than the ones he threw on me during his stories.

Walking away, I heard my uncle. "Someone's gotta talk to him."

Then my dad. "Let 'im find his own truth."

DINNER

My cousins Maria, Fat Tony and Crazy Gingy went to a different high school than my sister and I, so by the age of fifteen, we rarely saw them. Uncle Gingy and Aunt Connie's barbecues dissipated in time. I moved to Manhattan after high school and was tending bar at a restaurant right across from Lincoln Center.

Before this night, I hadn't seen my Aunt Connie in nine years. She came into Manhattan with three of her friends to see the New York City Ballet. She was still so pretty, still looking younger than she was.

"Aunt Connie! Oh, my God, you found me!"

She landed a serious Italian-aunt-from-Yonkers hug and kiss on me, then wiped the lipstick off my face.

"Your father told me you were working here."

"Don't go tellin' the whole neighborhood."

"Too long to not see my nephew. Look at you, you're all grown up and beautiful." She hugged me again. "These are my friends. Girls, this is my nephew, Joey."

One of the women was a neighbor, Joanne, who remembered me from the family barbecues when I was nine. They showed up with the rest of the pretheater crowd and had a fast dinner. I was slammed behind the bar, so we didn't get much chance to talk to each other, just asked how the family was.

As they were headed out to the show, I said, "Aunt Connie, I gotta tell ya, I miss those Nepperhan Avenue barbecues."

"Yeah. Me, too. Maybe someday. This time with grandchildren."

I said, "Don't look at me."

I gave Aunt Connie a big hug and kiss goodbye and one of her friends perked up and said, "Hey, do I get one of those, too?"

I obliged. Then another one said, "What about me?"

I wound up hugging and kissing all four of them.

"You made their month," my aunt said. Then she grabbed my face. "He's so cute."

BALLET

I was counting the money when someone knocked on the door. I walked over and saw Aunt Connie waving at me through the glass.

"Are you still open?" she asked.

"Yeah, come on in."

I locked the door behind her. She took a few steps in and looked around.

"Oh, you're closing up. Maybe I should just go and let you get out of here."

"No it's OK, I still have to Z-out—I mean, count the money."

"I'll just stay for a minute."

"Really, it's OK."

"I just haven't seen you in so long, so . . ."

"Listen, it's no problem. My bar is your bar. You want another glass of wine?"

"Yes. I would love one."

"Sit down." I jumped behind the bar. "Did you all go out after the show?"

"For a little while."

"What happened to your friends?"

"Um, they're on a train. Back to Yonkers. They went home."

"Oh. OK."

I didn't ask for an explanation to that. She settled on a stool and I poured her a glass of chardonnay.

"This tastes so good. We don't have it in the house anymore. So, how is it for you down here, Joey?"

"I love it, actually."

"This restaurant treating you well?"

"Affords me a place in Hell's Kitchen. Small, but it's all I need, really."

"You have a girlfriend?"

"Technically?"

"I don't wanna know."

"Good."

"Look at you. I can't believe how old you are. It's sort of blowing my mind. You look like you should be an actor. I mean, look at that face."

"You sound like my mom. You guys won't stop until I can't fit my head through the door. I didn't know you were such a fan of the ballet."

She cracked the saddest-looking smile. "You didn't know I was a dancer?"

"No."

"Well, I was. A ballet dancer."

"Are you serious?"

"Well, I was. What's the matter, you can't see it?"

"No, I just . . . I never heard that before."

"It's true. Just picture me thirty years and maybe thirty pounds ago and then you can see the next great ballerina hopeful from the Bronx."

"Yeah, OK, now that you mention it, I can see it."

"I danced from when I was a little girl. My parents had tutu pictures of me all over the house. You would laugh. Thank God my mother couldn't have any more children, otherwise my parents could never have afforded my lessons. They were so great. My father loved to watch me dance, rest his soul. I went to the High School of Music and Art. What a big deal that was. A girl from the Bronx going to high school in Manhattan? To study ballet? Are you kidding me? I was like a weirdo. You know that high school?"

"That's the one in the movie *Fame,* right?"

"That's right, that was me. I was gonna live forever."

"Were you gonna light up the sky like a flame?"

"Yes, I was. When I went there, the school was on Forty-sixth Street, Times Square, now it's, like, two blocks from here. On Amsterdam."

"You must have been really good."

"I was . . . yeah. I was good."

"Why'd you stop?"

"Ballet is really competitive. I mean, if you aren't good enough to start your career at sixteen, chances are you won't really have one. They'll make you graduate high school a year early so you can start working in your prime years. I didn't have the stuff that those girls did, the ones who went to Europe when they were sixteen to start their career."

"A career is one thing, but why'd you stop dancing at all?"

"Yeah, that's a good question. Well . . . I met your Uncle Gingy . . . we started dating. He's not one for classical arts. He only goes as far back as Jimmy Roselli. He . . . he didn't like the guys with their hands all over the girls. Their hands all over *me*. He just didn't get it."

She started laughing really hard. She couldn't even talk.

"He said . . . oh, God, I'll never forget. He came to see me dance once, and he said, 'Why does there have to be so many love scenes? Every scene is like a love scene. Actors don't even do that many love scenes. I mean, those guys, are they faggots or regular guys?' "

She continued to laugh. "He was so funny. He just didn't get it. He tried, though. He just had a real problem with it."

"That's too bad."

"And Uncle Gingy, more than anything, wanted a family. And so did I, really. So many people were getting married at that time. Me and your uncle, your parents, my Cousin Lucille. And we all got married around the same time. At the same place, too. There was this hall called Alex and Henry's. We had a wedding a year for five years in that place. It was the thing to do. Joey, your uncle was some charmer. He and your father both. Like you."

"Stop that."

"They always looked sharp. One thing those guys knew was how to dress."

"Yeah, when their mother finally stopped doing it for them."

She either ignored or missed that one. She stopped for a moment, slipped into her head and worked over a thought. She didn't share with me, but it made her smile to herself.

"Joey, could I have another glass of wine?"

"Sure."

"It's Saturday night, right?"

"Absolutely."

Aunt Connie looked out the front windows of the restaurant across the street to the Metropolitan Opera House. The huge fountain in front was lit up.

"You know, your mother and I used to be really close when she was still married to your father. I miss her."

"Yeah, she always asks about you."

"Tell her I was asking after her."

"I will."

"You know . . . it's not what everybody thinks."

"What's not?"

She gave me a look that said, *Come on, you know exactly what I'm talking about.* And I did.

"He really has changed. Of course, this whole Jesus thing is a friggin' pain in the ass. I'm sorry, excuse my language," she said to the ceiling. "I mean, it's sometimes difficult to understand. He is a little obsessive about a lot of things. Like church. He says if he misses one day of church, then that's a step back into his old ways. I actually miss some of his old ways. Now we can't have certain kinds of food in the house, the kids can't listen to the music. How could music be evil? And I don't even want to talk about the other things we can't do. I mean, if God gave us sex only so we could have children, don't you think this world would be a little over-populated? I just don't understand it, for Christ's sake. Is it me?"

"I don't think so."

"Me neither." Then, without hiding her melancholy, she said, "I just feel so heavy sometimes." I didn't know what to say to that. I waited for the follow-up, but she just tried to cover the awkward moment with a little sarcasm. "And Joey, don't you know if you have too much extra weight, then you can't fit through the eye of the needle into heaven?"

I played along by laughing. "You're not fat."

"I don't mean that kind of heavy."

"What kind, then?"

She was done with that subject. Looked away, took a sip.

"I really think you can be an actor or something, Joey. And you should start tonight. I mean, trust me, it goes fast. How old are you, twenty-four?"

"Good memory."

"I've got twenty-some-odd years on you and it only feels like a weekend."

I didn't know that, after this night, I wouldn't see Aunt Connie until six years later. It would be at my sister's wedding, where she and I wouldn't talk that much. We would dance. A slow one. We'd say nothing about this night. She'd ask me about my mom. I'd ask her how everything was, she'd say good, and we'd keep dancing.

JUST ONE MINUTE

When the money was downstairs in the safe and the wine was finished, it was time to go. When we stepped out of the restaurant, the fountains in front of the opera house had been turned off. My aunt mostly looked at the sidewalk when we hugged, and kept her head down as I walked away. I got half a block away and she yelled to me.

"Why are you walking that way?"

"What?"

"Don't go that way, don't do that!"

I walked back toward her.

"You want me to walk you to the train?"

"No."

"What, then?"

"Come here. Come back here."

I kept going until we were in touching distance.

"I thought you said you wanted to walk to the train by yourself."

"I know what I said. Forget the train. I've already been on the train. I got on with my friends. They think I went to the bathroom in the next car. Forget it, forget everything I said. I'm so heavy, Joey."

She started crying.

"You OK, Aunt Connie?"

"Why are you making me do this? I don't want to be the one who does this."

"Does what?"

"I know you're not stupid, Joey."

"I don't understand."

"Just fucking put your fucking hands on me, what the fuck is wrong with you?"

"What?"

"I can't say that again. Just please just do it, please!"

I stepped over and cautiously gave her a little hug.

"Not like that. You're gonna make me do *this,* too?" She reached behind her and grabbed my wrist. "Like this."

She pressed my hand down between her breasts.

"Come on," she said. And undid a button of her blouse. She pushed herself against me so hard I had to contort my arm to get my hand under her bra. She leaned all her weight into me until I was holding her off the ground—one hand around her waist, one on her breast.

"Hold me up for just a minute. Just for one goddamn minute."

CANCELLED

CANCELLED